MISSING PERSON

"So you met her *here?*" another of the officers asked.

"No," April said, with a big sigh. "I didn't meet her here. But she *said* she was coming here. That was the last thing she told me."

"So you don't know if she actually came here that day?"

"No," April replied, grimly.

A heavy wave of hopelessness suddenly overwhelmed her. Her patience with the cops' questions was beginning to wear thin, revealing the truer emotion underneath it. It was the feeling she had been trying, for weeks now, to avoid: raw despair. That was the exact moment she heard a voice from inside the small crowd of onlookers.

"I saw her," the voice said.

It was a man's voice. April and the police officers, and a few stragglers standing around in front of Metropolitan Bakery, suddenly turned around to see who'd spoken. Before April spotted the man, she saw the faces of the people who had seen him: the looks were of startled surprise, curiosity, even amusement. And then she saw what they saw. A young Amish man, with wide shoulders and long limbs, stepped confidently forward.

BOOK YOUR PLACE ON OUR WEBSITE AND MAKE THE READING CONNECTION!

We've created a customized website just for our very special readers, where you can get the inside scoop on everything that's going on with Zebra, Pinnacle and Kensington books.

When you come online, you'll have the exciting opportunity to:
- View covers of upcoming books
- Read sample chapters
- Learn about our future publishing schedule (listed by publication month and author)
- Find out when your favorite authors will be visiting a city near you
- Search for and order backlist books from our online catalog
- Check out author bios and background information
- Send e-mail to your favorite authors
- Meet the Kensington staff online
- Join us in weekly chats with authors, readers and other guests
- Get writing guidelines
- AND MUCH MORE!

**Visit our website at
http://www.kensingtonbooks.com**

SEARCHING
FOR ROSE

DANA BECKER

ZEBRA BOOKS
KENSINGTON PUBLISHING CORP.
www.kensingtonbooks.com

ZEBRA BOOKS are published by

Kensington Publishing Corp.
119 West 40th Street
New York, NY 10018

All Kensington titles, imprints, and distributed lines are available at special quantity discounts for bulk purchases for sales promotion, premiums, fund-raising, educational, or institutional use.

Special book excerpts or customized printings can also be created to fit specific needs. For details, write or phone the office of the Kensington Sales Manager: Attn.: Sales Department. Kensington Publishing Corp., 119 West 40th Street, New York, NY 10018. Phone: 1-800-221-2647.

Zebra and the Z logo Reg. U.S. Pat. & TM Off.
BOUQUET Reg. U.S. Pat. & TM Off.

First Printing: September 2020
ISBN-13: 978-1-4201-5188-6
ISBN-10: 1-4201-5188-6

ISBN-13: 978-1-4201-5189-3 (eBook)
ISBN-10: 1-4201-5189-4 (eBook)

10 9 8 7 6 5 4 3 2 1

Printed in the United States of America

Chapter One

April wasn't the type to call the cops. She took care of her own business, didn't need to rely on anyone. That, at least, was the story she liked to tell about herself. But here she was, standing at the bustling center of Reading Terminal Market in downtown Philadelphia, talking openly with two uniformed officers as a small crowd of curious on-lookers gathered around.

She was trying to explain, for the hundredth time, what had happened: her sister, Rose, was gone.

"What do you mean 'gone'?" one of the cops asked.

"*Gone*," April replied, already regretting this conversation. "As in *disappeared*."

Nobody had heard from Rose in about two weeks. She hadn't shown up to her job at Walgreens. She had, by all appearances, vanished into thin air. Wasn't it difficult enough for April to deal with this emotionally? Why did she have to explain it, too?

And there were things April wasn't saying. Things she'd barely admit to herself, much less tell the police. But here's what she did reveal: her sister's last words to her, before she disappeared. *I'm going to Reading. I'm going to that bakery*. Well, April was now at Reading Terminal Market, at that bakery, doing her part. She was talking to the cops, trying to make them understand.

"So you met her *here?*" another of the officers asked.

"No," April said, with a big sigh. "I didn't meet her here. But she *said* she was coming here. That was the last thing she told me."

"So you don't know if she actually came here that day?"

"No," April replied, grimly.

A heavy wave of hopelessness suddenly overwhelmed her. Her patience with the cops' questions was beginning to wear thin, revealing the truer emotion underneath it. It was the feeling she had been trying, for weeks now, to avoid: raw despair. That was the exact moment she heard a voice from inside the small crowd of onlookers.

"I saw her," the voice said.

It was a man's voice. April and the police officers, and a few stragglers standing around in front of Metropolitan Bakery, suddenly turned around to see who'd spoken. Before April spotted the man, she saw the faces of the people who had seen him: the looks were of startled surprise, curiosity, even amusement. And then she saw what they saw. A young Amish man, with wide shoulders and long limbs, stepped confidently forward. April had seen him before, around the market, but never up close.

"Yes," he said, pointing to the photo that one of the officers was holding in his hand. "*Her,*" he continued. "I remember seeing her. I saw her last week."

For a moment, nobody, not even the police, said a word, as though waiting to hear what else the man might have to say. But, for the moment, he said nothing more.

The cops eyed him warily, skeptically.

"You sure?" one of the officers said.

"Yes," the Amish man replied. "I am certain."

And he really did seem certain. As he answered the officers' questions, April watched him closely. When they asked his name, he turned to April, as though addressing *her,* looked deeply at her, and said, "Joseph. Joseph Young." He pronounced his own name as though he were delivering a piece of dramatic news. To April, that's exactly how it felt.

His demeanor was unlike anything she'd ever seen in a man. Especially in one her own age. He seemed entirely in control, but without the need to assert his control over the situation. He held immense power in his large body but didn't bother wielding it, didn't seem to feel the need to show off. He seemed even more powerful for his restraint, more charismatic for his ability to master his charisma. To the police, he delivered strong, clear answers that were direct and sincere. He answered with a crisp "yes," never "yeah" or "yup." He wasn't trying to conceal something or compensate for anything. He was, in short, perfectly comfortable in his skin.

And what a skin it was. This man was head-turningly handsome. His serious face allowed for a quick smile, and April noticed he had dimples.

April was noticing, too, that she wasn't the only one seeing this. The eyes of the cops, and everyone who lingered in front of the bakery, were glued to this strange, beautiful man. Nobody wanted to interrupt him or let him go. Unless it was her imagination, it seemed that the cops were now only asking him questions as an excuse to keep him in front of their eyes.

And then there was his gaze. At various moments, he looked directly at April with intense green eyes—but why was he so interested in her? Maybe it was because she was the sister of the missing girl. Or was it because April herself was staring at him? Could it be because he was as taken with her as she was with him? Whatever the reason, the effect of that gaze on April was immediate, and it registered bodily. It felt as if she was standing in the hot beam of a theater spotlight. It was the same sensation she'd felt when she used to act in school plays. And, just as his eyes warmed her skin like hot stage lights, she felt the need to perform, to make a speech, to undertake some grand gesture—and increasingly the gesture she wanted to make was a dramatic exit. The heat was too much. She needed to do something, anything, not to seem like a deer caught in the headlights.

But the more April watched him, and the more she detected how intensely controlled he was, the more she also sensed that he was, just maybe, a bit too controlled. He would be hard to reach. A fortress. An impressive fortress, no doubt. But a fortress.

So mesmerized was April by this man that she hardly noticed that the police had stopped talking to him and had turned back to her, with some additional questions. She tried her best to focus on what she was being asked. But, in doing so, she lost track of the beautiful man. And before she knew it, when she looked around, he was nowhere to be seen.

That was the first time April paid close attention to the mysterious Joseph Young. But it wasn't the first time he'd studied her. In fact, he'd had his eye on her from the moment she'd made a dramatic entrance at the bakery in Reading Terminal Market almost a week earlier.

Joseph had witnessed the whole scene that day. From his own corner of Reading Terminal Market, at the Amish-run diner next to the bakery, he'd watched it unfold. That day, a Friday, he could tell that something was very wrong even before he knew what it was. He sensed trouble. And he wasn't the only one. The bakery's owner, Carmen, also sensed it.

Standing at her shop counter, carefully arranging the day's assorted delicacies—brioches and tartes Tatin, fresh out of the oven—Carmen sensed a commotion outside the bakery, somewhere out in the sprawling mass of Reading Terminal Market, which was packed with crowds shopping for a summer weekend. Carmen and Joseph, both, detected it as a minor disturbance of air, like the early breezes of an impending storm.

Just as Carmen rose to her tiptoes to peer over the crowd and investigate the situation, April lunged out of the mass of people, elbowing her way forward— seeming, as Carmen would later remember it, as though she weren't walking but somehow spinning, like a drunk ballerina pirouetting wildly. April sped headlong through the doorway of Carmen's bakery, tripped over one of the café chairs, and braced her body against the counter. Joseph, who happened to be standing nearby, saw this and followed her into the shop, where he witnessed the whole exchange.

"I need your phone," April had said, staring directly at Carmen. "I gotta make a call."

April was not blinking.

Carmen drew a long, loud breath through her nose.

"Sorry, hon," she said, straightening her back. "Can't do that."

Carmen wasn't from Philadelphia. But she'd lived there long enough, almost twenty years now, that she'd seen all of the mischief and misery the city had to offer. Half of the city, it seemed, *needed* her phone, or something of hers, at some point. Did a day go by when someone on the street didn't try to hustle her out of something?

Carmen quickly sized up the young woman standing in front of her. To survive in the city, a pretty girl like this would have to project an aura of danger. High and tight ponytail, hoop earrings, fire engine red lipstick to contrast with straight black hair and green eyes, high-waisted slightly baggy jeans, ripped at the knees and dotted with flecks of paint, red Air Jordans on her feet, a short, purple-black faux leather jacket, and a grimy fraying gray T-shirt. Philly was full of young women like her, Carmen thought. They're tough, sure, but mostly they want you to think they're tough. In other words: they're hiding something. Carmen tried to remain unmoved.

What gave her pause was the look on the young woman's face, the same look that had brought Joseph into the shop behind her: it was a look of genuine distress.

A memory flashed in Carmen's mind. Childhood. The farm. *That girl.*

Carmen came from country folk, who only went to hospitals if they needed surgery. Otherwise they used their own home remedies. Once, when she was really young, maybe eight or nine, she'd seen the most awful thing. Without any warning or previous sign of illness, a teenaged neighbor girl dropped dead one day while doing her chores in the dairy. Within days, the family buried the poor girl in the family plot. There was only one problem: she wasn't dead.

She'd fallen prey to a rare form of catatonia,

which closely mimicked signs of death. When they'd checked for a heartbeat, they didn't hear it because the beats were so faint and so infrequent that her heart truly might not have been beating during the moments when they listened. She was, to all appearances, dead. And so they buried her.

The girl's younger brother, however, was so distraught at her loss that he'd spent all of his free time at her graveside, refusing to believe that she was gone. Incredibly, he heard clawing sounds from her tomb, and set out desperately to dig her out. In the end, they rescued her. But she was never the same.

Carmen had seen the girl after she'd been unburied. She remembered seeing her walk around town, at the market, so skinny, and with this doomed look on her face. Could the girl speak? She must have spoken. But Carmen never once heard her say even a single word. A ghost of a ghost.

She rarely thought about the unburied girl from her childhood. But that girl, her face, came to Carmen suddenly when she saw this stranger—the look in her eyes—as she leaned against the bakery counter. The memory came with a startlingly vivid flash.

"Phone," April was saying, almost panting. "*Please*."

Carmen felt her defenses weakening.

"What's the matter, sweetheart?"

"My sister, she's . . ." said the girl, in an odd, absent sort of way, "*gone*."

Carmen retreated into the back to find her phone. As she rummaged through her purse, she saw April standing at the bakery counter, eating the bread samples, ravenously, until the plate was empty.

Why me? Carmen thought, then felt a bit guilty.

When Carmen returned to the counter, April was in tears. She was holding a photo of her missing sister, printed on a piece of office paper.

"This is the most recent one I got," she said. "Have you seen her? Her name is Rose. She comes around here a lot."

"Here?"

"*Here*," April said, "to this bakery."

"Oh," said Carmen, feeling a sudden knot in her throat. "I see."

She examined the photo. The missing girl had boy-short, bright red hair and big, mischievous eyes. She appeared to be a bit younger and a bit more punk than April. In the picture she was shown in a booth at a Chili's, intentionally leaning in front of another girl, impishly blocking her out of the photo. Her mouth was slightly open.

"What was she saying?" Carmen suddenly asked.

"Saying?" said April.

"Yeah," Carmen replied, handing the photo back to April. "In the picture. It looks like she's saying something."

April looked at the photo and smiled a tiny bit. "Probably something dumb."

"Well, she does look familiar, I think. That red hair," Carmen said. "But I can't remember when I might have seen her last. Not this week, I don't think."

Carmen handed her phone to April. She wiped her hands on her jeans, pulled out a piece of paper with a number on it, and began furiously dialing.

"I'm calling her friend," she said to Carmen. And then, a moment later: "*Ugh.*" There was no answer. She left a breathless message.

Uh, hey, it's me . . . I'm calling from someone's phone because mine got cut off. Look, Rose's gone. I don't know where she is. I haven't heard from her for more than three days. You know she's not like that. I'm really scared. I don't need to tell you what I'm afraid of. I know you know. I'm at Reading now. Please call me back at this number or come here as soon as you can. I'm at . . .

She turned to Carmen.

"Metropolitan Bakery," Carmen said.

The Metropolitan Bakery, April said into the phone. *Reading Terminal Market.*

April put the phone back on the counter and looked helplessly at Carmen.

"I think you should call the police, hon," Carmen said.

"*No,*" April replied with a vehemence that startled Carmen.

"I just think . . ."

"I'm *not* calling the police."

"Okay, hon," Carmen said. "Just keep it in mind, okay?"

* * *

For the next few hours April waited in the bakery, sitting at the table next to the door, staring out into the marketplace. Carmen made her a sandwich, which the girl at first ignored and then, in four rapid bites, devoured. At noon, when the bakery got crowded, a young woman about April's age approached her table and, seeing that she'd finished her meal, asked if April was about to leave. With teeth clenched in rage, April said loudly, "How about you keep walking." Carmen overheard this, sighed, dropped a croissant on a plate, walked briskly over to April's table, and slid the croissant in front of her.

"You will *not* talk to my customers like that," she said. "I'm running a business here."

April glared at her.

"Do you understand? Answer me."

"Yeah," April said. "I got it."

Even as Carmen handled long lines of customers, she'd turn an eye toward April. For hours, the girl sat in the same spot, almost motionless, just staring. Occasionally, she would stand up, look intently out the window, as though recognizing someone, and begin to walk toward the door, only to discover that it wasn't the person she thought, and then retreat back to her seat.

Joseph Young had watched all of this from afar. Whenever possible, he'd drift over toward the bakery, to see what was happening with the girl whose sister was missing. He considered going up to her and saying something. But what? And anyway, she seemed agitated, and not in the mood for company. Joseph decided to let her be—for now. But he was keeping an eye on her.

By the end of the day, April was still sitting there. As Carmen began to mop the floor, April suddenly jumped up.

"I gotta go," she said and made for the door.

"Wait!" Carmen called out. "What if your friend calls me back?"

"She's not my friend," April said over her shoulder.

And then she was gone, swallowed up in the crowded market. On her way out, she'd walked right past Joseph, who had drifted back toward the door of the bakery—possibly for the twentieth time that day—to keep watch over April. In her haste, she had bumped into him, and the contact had jolted him far more than he expected. The aroma of her perfume had reached him quickly and lingered powerfully for a moment before thinning out into the ether. Its fragrance was unmistakable. As Joseph watched April disappear, he named it aloud, letting the word pass over his lips like a gently felt secret.

Roses, he whispered.

Joseph had been so antsy to see April that he barely slept. But April did not show up at all the next morning, or during lunch. By 3:00 P.M. Joseph was losing hope. By 5:00 P.M., he was fairly certain he'd never see her again.

Carmen, too, was preoccupied with thoughts of this troubled young stranger. On her postwork walk home, Carmen kept her eyes wide open, looking for April's missing sister—but she was also looking for April herself. The search went on for two days. During this time, Carmen called and re-called the number April had dialed, but never got a response. Had it all been a dream? Maybe April and her missing sister were just figments of her imagination?

But then, on Monday morning, shortly after opening time, as Carmen set out a display of fresh rosemary rolls—and Joseph was fielding the breakfast crowd over at the Amish diner—April was suddenly back, standing at the bakery counter, helping herself to samples, gobbling up little bits of bread as though she hadn't eaten anything in days.

"Hey there," Carmen said, trying to act casual. She slid a plate with a cranberry-walnut roll on it to April. "It's hot out of the oven. Want some butter?"

April nodded.

"Any luck with your sister?" Carmen said as she buttered the roll.

"Her name is Rose," April said. "And no."

"Have you considered calling the cops?"

"Not doing it," April said, with a mouth full of bread.

"Listen," Carmen whispered, leaning over the counter, "the cops are going to find out that there's a missing person. And if they find out you knew and didn't report it, they're going to suspect *you*."

Carmen had no idea what she was talking about. Everything she knew about police procedure came from TV and movies. But it didn't stop her from speaking confidently. She figured the kid needed a push.

"You listen to me. You're gonna have to deal with cops, one way or the other," Carmen found herself saying, mimicking the shows she watched. "The question is: you gonna be the worried sister or a suspect? Your choice."

April nodded slowly.

"I'll think about it."

"Good," Carmen said, switching back into her real voice. "Now . . . how are *you* doing?"

"Me?" April said, and made a sound that was either a laugh or a whimper—Carmen couldn't tell. "I'm a complete and total mess."

April told Carmen a story that made her head spin. April was doing a court-ordered Narcotics Anonymous program; if she missed any NA meetings without a good excuse, it was over for her. She would be immediately arrested and forced to serve six to twelve months in prison. The judge who'd ordered it had literally pointed at April and said, "Don't mess up this time, or you're going to find yourself in a tiny prison cell. I promise you that."

The words had chilled April to the bone. She'd had a lot of run-ins with the law, from drug possession charges to small-theft charges. So far, she'd managed to avoid jail time. But her luck was running out and she lived in deep fear of prison.

"I can't go there," she told Carmen. "I know what goes on in there. I got friends who've told me. And

I'm claustrophobic. I can't be in a locked room. I can't do it. I'll go insane."

But, at this point, April was in the system. And being in the system meant there was a force as strong as gravity pulling her toward prison. She hadn't missed any meetings yet, or the community service that she had to do, but she'd been very close a few times. She'd passed the first urine test. But it had been a huge battle for her. She didn't think she'd be able to keep up for six months.

"And it's not just 'cause I'm messed up," April told Carmen. "I mean, okay, I *am* messed up, right? But it's more than just that."

Last week, for example, April had had a chance to get a job—making sandwiches at a Subway—but the manager had wanted her to start on a night when she had to do community service work and he wasn't willing to be flexible. So she lost that chance. And another prospective employer, in another shop, almost physically kicked her out when she said that she'd have to work around her NA meetings and community service work. A temp agency laughed in her face when she arrived underdressed and without a resume. April was broke and becoming desperate.

"I don't know what I'm doing wrong," April said.

Everything, Carmen thought to herself. *You are doing everything wrong.*

And then, of course, there were her problems with men. April had a type: beautiful boys, who were incompetent criminals. And who were just generally incompetent. "This kid didn't even know how to tie his shoes," April told Carmen of her last boyfriend.

Carmen snorted.

"I'm serious, though," April said. "He literally didn't know how to do it right. I taught him Bunny Ears. Like I'm his momma. He got mad at me when I did it but then he totally used it."

He also didn't know how to put on his sweatshirt. He would struggle inside of it, like a chick trying to hatch from an egg. April used to watch the process with amusement. It had endeared him to her. She was charmed to see this tough guy vulnerable for a moment. But, later in their relationship, when things had gotten bad, she was far less amused.

He'd developed a pill addiction that ravaged his body, his mind, his life, and, eventually, April's life, too. Her first major court case came from her involvement with him: she was caught helping him break into a house—the house of his best friend's mother, no less—to steal some jewelry and electronics to sell to support the habit. April had figured that, if she helped him, he was less likely to get caught. Instead, she was the one who got caught.

Carmen listened quietly to everything April was telling her. Suddenly, without thinking, she said, "How would you like a job here at the bakery?"

Even as the words were coming out of her mouth, she found herself thinking: *What am I* saying? *Someone tells me 'I'm an addict and a felon' and my response is 'Hey, come work for me'?* Carmen was beginning to doubt her sanity.

But she'd made the offer, and April's response, she had to admit, was rather winning. April ran around the counter and threw her arms around Carmen's neck.

"You don't know how much this means," she said, as she hugged Carmen. "I'm gonna work *really* hard. Not gonna let you down."

Carmen really wanted to believe it.

April was late to work the next morning. And, the next day, she arrived even later. After a week, it was official: April was incapable of arriving on time. Each morning, she had an excuse. Of course, Joseph, watching from afar, didn't mind. He was just thrilled that April was suddenly working only a hundred feet away from him. It seemed like a gift.

Carmen didn't mind April's constant lateness either—she was just worried about what it meant: what other problems April might bring to the bakery.

The ongoing situation with Rose's disappearance made Carmen very nervous. What kind of mess was that? At the end of the workweek, April had finally called the cops to report the disappearance. Carmen had made it a condition of her working at the bakery— but she still didn't know the exact reason April had been so uptight about the police to begin with. Was April concerned about her own legal problems or was there something more? Carmen wanted to know the answer, but she also really, really did *not* want to know. She didn't want to hear something that would pull her deeper into whatever kind of mess this was.

Carmen watched, nervously, as April made the rounds in Reading Terminal Market, chatting with the market's shopkeepers about her missing sister, asking them to help keep a lookout, and giving them an official "Missing" poster. Carmen wanted to help with the search, too. But every time she saw April, wearing a Metropolitan Bakery apron—which April had done intentionally so she would be taken more seriously for these little meetings—Carmen winced. All around the market, April's troubles, whatever they were, were becoming synonymous with the bakery and, by extension, with Carmen herself. Carmen knew these shopkeepers well, and she knew that they would want no part of whatever kind of trouble was behind Rose's disappearance. She knew that they, like Carmen herself, worried that this mess would eventually intrude on their businesses.

One afternoon—the day before the police had come to take April's statement—Carmen noticed April standing by the door, watching something outside the bakery.

"Come here," April said, motioning to Carmen. "Check this out."

Carmen and April watched a young, tall Amish man posting Rose's "Missing" posters on a wall across the way, next to the Amish diner. They watched as he posted another one on the door to the market itself. And on a pillar in the middle of the market. And, then, on another door. The Amish man, in fact, had an entire stack of "Missing" signs under his arm, and he was posting as many as he could, on any surface he could find.

Carmen sighed.

"April . . ."

"I had nothing to do with this!" April said. "I didn't even talk to the Amish diner people about Rose. I have no idea where he got the signs."

Carmen gave April a skeptical look.

"I'm serious," said April. "I didn't say a word to them. I'm kind of afraid of them."

Carmen and April watched for a few more moments as the man continued to cover the market with pictures of Rose.

"I mean, I didn't say anything to them *before,*" April said, breaking the silence. "But I guess now . . . I will? I mean, that guy's weirdly cute, don't you think?"

Carmen rolled her eyes and drifted over to the bakery counter. "Back to work, kiddo," she shouted from behind a pile of bread loaves.

Chapter Two

The hand-painted NICK'S REPAIR sign was so faded that nobody driving by on Route 23 would notice it hanging there. But it didn't much matter. Nick's Repair already had all the customers it needed, and they knew exactly where to find it.

Even though April was ninety-five percent certain that the shop was connected to Rose's disappearance, she wasn't sure what, exactly, she was looking for when she'd set out on an almost two-hour bus ride from Philly that took her to a random stop just west of Lancaster, Pennsylvania. For most of the morning, she'd just stood outside of Nick's, across the two-lane highway, behind a bush, and watched.

She didn't see too many trucks go in. Those that entered, didn't stay long. Nobody, from what she could tell, was actually going to the shop to have their truck repaired—this fit what she already knew about the place: that it was a truck repair shop in name only.

Rose, too, had known this. And this bit of information was the reason for her sudden disappearance—

at least, April suspected as much. For almost three years, Rose had dated the co-owner of this shop, a man named Ricky Devereux. Ricky was the kind of guy who liked to tell people that he was an "independent businessman," without specifying what kind of business. And he always made a point of handing out a business card, whether or not the occasion warranted it. It had been a running joke between Rose and April. Especially when April discovered that the card read "Richard J. Devereux" on it.

"*Richard?* Ha!" April had said when she'd seen the card. "That guy's a 'Ricky' all the way."

Any time she'd wanted to make her sister giggle, April would adopt an over-the-top posh English accent, curtsey, and say, "Charmed to make your acquaintance, Sir Richard."

But it wasn't long before Rose and Ricky became more serious as a couple and April had to tone down her mockery. Despite the chaos of her own love life, or perhaps because of it, April had a difficult time watching Rose grow closer to a man she considered a lowlife, who offered her beloved sister only heartache, and possibly also serious trouble. April's efforts to advise Rose—sometimes tactfully, usually not—to break up with Ricky, had become a constant source of tension between the inseparable sisters.

Once, when Rose had asked her, "What's so bad about him?" April had lost her temper and begun shouting.

"Um, lemme see . . . well, first of all, he's a lying-piece-of-trash-grease-monkey-thug. And that's just *one* thing. Want me to name others?"

After these outbursts, the sisters would stop talking for a bit, usually for about a week, but sometimes for as long as a month. This was the reason April hadn't, at first, realized that Rose was missing—they'd recently had another fight over Ricky.

Still, the sisters' bond was unshakable. They not only reconciled after fights, they continued to confide in each other completely. Rose never concealed the things she'd learned about Ricky, and they weren't pretty. He was involved in a racket which, from what Rose could tell, had grown from a small indiscretion here and there into a full-fledged criminal operation that had turned a once-legitimate truck repair business—founded twenty years earlier by Ricky's father, Nick—into a front.

Having grown up in the shop, Ricky had made deep connections among the teamsters whose trucks he repaired. Occasionally he'd hook them up with some pills. Aderall for alertness. But also prescription painkillers like Vicodin and OxyContin. He'd done this mostly as favors, as a friend who knew how tough it was out there on the road. The truckers trusted him completely, and vice versa.

But when Ricky's brother-in-law, Dylan, joined the shop, and eventually became a co-owner after Nick died, things changed. Dylan was a shrewd businessman and he also happened to have absolutely no scruples. He realized that their teamster clientele was not only an excellent market for pills but that the truckers could serve as a reliable delivery service for what he imagined could be, and eventually became, a major cross-country smuggling operation. Instead of fixing trucks and handing out pills as small favors to their best clients, Nick's Repair became primarily a drug operation that fixed trucks as favors, and as a front.

Rose had learned about all of this from Ricky, who'd begun to have much more money to throw around and had also become increasingly anxious about getting caught. He'd needed someone to confide in and that person was Rose. April had long feared that this knowledge would lead to major trouble for her sister (and even for her—she'd stopped talking to Rose about Ricky's work over the phone, for fear that someone, Dylan or the police, might be listening in).

Rose had become increasingly agitated and suspicious. April could tell that something terrible had happened—something that Rose refused to tell her. Rose gave hints that cops, maybe even the feds, were tracing Dylan and Ricky, and that she might have to testify against them or risk a serious penalty herself. She wouldn't elaborate. Not because she didn't trust April but because she didn't want to implicate her. She was trying to be a good sister. And then, suddenly, she disappeared.

That was what brought April out to Nick's Repair that day, to watch, to try to gather whatever information she could. But as it became more and more clear that April wasn't going to learn anything new by hiding in a bush and staking out the shop, she faced a decision: go inside or leave.

But just as she began to call a car to take her back to the bus station, she changed her mind. She needed to be brave if she was going to find Rose. If these guys knew something about where her sister was—where she'd been for weeks now—it meant they were the ones to talk to, even if they were dangerous. What choice did she have? For all she knew, Rose was right here, somewhere in that shop.

The thought of her sister being so close by . . . just the thought of it clutched at April's heart. She hadn't quite felt their separation physically until then, hadn't quite admitted, even to herself, how much she missed her sister.

April marched toward the shop. She reminded herself to be watchful for any clues. The first one came the moment she pushed the door open. The body language of the two men sitting in the shop sent a clear message: guilt. Guilty of what, April didn't know. But these guys were undeniably hiding something. One of the men, sitting at a dingy desk, tensed up; the other, who was sitting on the desk, jumped off as though he were about to spring into action. Instead, he folded his arms over his large chest. He was a massive man. She immediately recognized him. Something in his face told her that he, too, recognized her.

"Yeah?" he said.

To which the other man, the one seated at the desk, added, "Whadayou? Lost?"

"No," April said.

"Well, we do repairs. You got a rig needs work?"

"Nope," April said.

The men exchanged a look.

"Have we met?" the desk guy said.

He squinted and leaned forward to get a better look at April in the dim light of the window-less shop. April stood in front of the door, within arm's reach of it. Just in case she needed to flee.

Now the standing man uncrossed his arms and wagged a finger insistently at April.

"Yeah, yeah," he said. "I know you! We met at the boss's. At a party. You're Rose's friend, right?"

"Sister," April said.

"Right!" he replied, and, turning to the other man, added, "Rose is the boss's chick."

"Ex," April interjected.

Both men gave April a look.

"Well," the desk guy said, "boss ain't in."

"My sister is missing," April said.

"We don't know nothing about that," the desk man said.

April's eyes narrowed, and the other man quickly added, "Sorry to hear that."

"Yeah," April said. "I agree. It's kind of a shame that my sister suddenly disappeared into thin air."

April was feeling strangely confident. Her instincts were telling her that these guys knew something about Rose's disappearance. She knew what this meant: that, by coming here, she was putting herself into greater danger. And yet . . . she was *doing* something. She was taking the initiative.

Without being conscious of it, she began to walk away from the safety of the door, her escape hatch, and drifted toward the men. April realized what was happening when she noticed the standing man gesture to the desk man, who opened a drawer and slipped his hand inside it. He didn't take anything out; he just sat there, with his hand in the drawer, his eyes glued to April.

"Like he said, boss isn't here," said the standing man, holding his hand up, making the *stop* gesture to April.

April stopped.

"Can I wait here for him?"

"No," the standing man said. "He's out of town. Not coming back 'til next week."

"When? I'll come back."

"I got a better idea. How about you leave him a message? Boss wants to talk to you, he'll call you."

"But I . . ."

"Hey," said the man, pointing to a notepad on the desk. "Just leave a message, and then move on. We got work to do here."

The cold air in the parking lot of Nick's Repair was spiked with diesel gas and burned rubber—but it smelled sweet to April. She was so relieved to be out of the shop, away from those men. She felt that she'd bested them in battle. She'd achieved what she'd set out to do: to probe Nick's Repair for clues. The men were nervous and defensive—this was a clue. They acted as though they didn't know Rose was missing—but they also didn't seem surprised. It was very easy to imagine that Ricky would have at least mentioned her disappearance to them. So why were they lying? What were they covering up? And, also, where *was* Ricky? Was he really "out of town"? The whole situation reeked.

She'd also achieved her second goal: to communicate a message to Ricky, with whom she hadn't spoken in probably half a year. Ricky was one of the last people who'd seen Rose before her disappearance. One way or the other, he was critical to April's search. Before she'd run out of the shop, April had scrawled out her phone number and a message:

Ricky—I haven't seen Rose in weeks. I need your help. Call me as soon as you read this. Ricky, I'm looking for Rose <u>on my own</u>. *But if you don't help me, I'm coming back here next time with friends.*

—April

It was a bold message. A threat. And it wasn't just about what she'd said in the note. It was about the larger message she'd sent just by walking into enemy territory, speaking confidently, and walking out with her head held high. It was about making her demands, without wavering, even as one of the men appeared to hold a gun under the table. April's message that day was clear enough: she was not afraid. Nor was she going to be intimidated. She was on a mission to find Rose and would not be deterred.

April rushed to the station and arrived just in time for the last bus back to Philly. She collapsed into her bus seat, by a window, near the back. For a minute it seemed she might get lucky and be the one person on the bus with an empty seat next to her. But just as the driver was about to close the door, another person jumped aboard. April's heart sank.

Oh, great, she thought as she closed her eyes.

Five predictable seconds later, she heard a tired man's voice asking her if the seat was free.

Perfect, she thought. *Some dude. Can't I catch any sort of break, ever?*

Hoping to set a tone of blistering indifference, April shrugged and mumbled, "Yeah, I guess."

Out of curiosity she opened her eyes a tiny bit, just to see what kind of degenerate she was dealing with. And instantly her entire attitude changed. Standing next to the seat—looking so tall, dark, and handsome that she almost laughed out loud—was the Amish guy from Reading Terminal Market, the one who'd been posting Rose's "Missing" posters everywhere, the one who'd testified to the police about seeing Rose in the market. He removed his wide-brimmed straw hat and held it to his chest; his strong forearm flexed in the process. All at once, she remembered how striking he'd been when she'd seen him talking to the police.

Now that her eyes were wide open and looking right at him, the Amish guy returned her gaze directly, with a warm, green look that was bold but not brash. Nobody, and certainly no man, had ever looked at her that way. She could feel her body expanding a bit, or lifting. Something, anyway, was pushing her physically in his direction.

"*Hi*," she said, realizing that she was smiling much too widely.

He suddenly became slightly shy—or rather, half his face, his mouth, lost its boldness, and tightened up. But his eyes, April noted, didn't avert their strong gaze.

"Uh, hello," he said with a deep nod.

Did he just bow at me? she thought. April was trying, and failing, not to giggle.

"I recognize you from Reading Market," she said. "I see you, like, every day there."

And when he just continued staring, she quickly added, "Do you recognize *me?*" She narrowed her eyes.

The Amish man nodded, sat down next to her, placed an adorably tiny piece of luggage under his seat, fixed his hat on top of it, sighed, and ran his big strong hands over his big, strong knees, straightening his pants.

Did he even hear what I just said? April thought.

Finally, after taking another deep breath, he replied,

"I do know you. You work at the bakery." He turned to her. "I see you, too."

This comment made her smile a bit too obviously, and she could feel herself blushing under his gaze.

"I've been meaning to thank you," she said. "For putting up those signs, for my sister, the missing girl. And for talking to the police like that."

"Oh," the man said gravely. "Well. We're praying for her."

"Thank you," April said. "That really means a lot to me." A wave of emotion suddenly overcame her. These waves came unexpectedly.

Just then, she looked down and realized, with horror, that she had the word *undies* scrawled on the back of her hand. Actually, it was more like *UNDIES!!* She'd written it there, while waiting for the bus, when she realized that she really needed to launder her underwear and that it couldn't wait another day. Unfortunately, it was on her left hand, the same hand that now faced Joseph. Had he seen it? Mortified, she quickly pulled her sweatshirt sleeve over her hand, and abruptly said, "I'm April, by the way."

"Like the month?"

"Exactly like that."

Omigod, is the Amish guy flirting with me? she thought.

"I'm Joseph."

"Yes, I know. Isn't that a guy in the Bible?"

"Yes," he said with a big smile. "But I'm not him."

Omigod, the Amish guy is definitely *flirting with me!* she thought, and immediately put herself on alert to stop smiling for at least a second or two.

They chatted for a bit. She learned about his background. He lived in Western Pennsylvania, in a little town called Sugar Grove. He often stayed with cousins who lived on the other side of the state, closer to Philly, so that he could help them at their farm and with their businesses in town, starting with the Amish-run diner across the way from Carmen's bakery. The idea was that he would learn how business was done in the big city and develop some know-how and some networks at Philly's farmers' markets, restaurants, and supermarkets. In the meantime, he was working in the Amish diner and in construction, saving money and learning the ropes. His dream—that was the word he used, *dream*—was to learn enough and save enough that eventually he could own a farm and break into the city's organic markets, especially eggs and dairy.

"Cheese," he said, simply. "Folks in town eat quite a bit of cheese."

People in Philly not only ate a lot of cheese, but they were happy to spend a lot of money for it. And they also loved buying Amish products—but there were almost no good Amish cheese lines. Joseph had a brother who'd moved to Wisconsin and done construction for some high-end cheesemakers, helping them build smokehouses, and he had learned a lot about the process. A good line of high-end Amish cheeses was, Joseph believed, an opening in the Philadelphia market.

But the cheese idea, too, was just a means to an even bigger goal: high-end furniture. That was his long-term goal: to design and build beautiful furniture. Joseph had built furniture his whole life. He'd learned the rudiments from his father and uncle—and during his walks around Philly, he'd seen all kinds of beautiful-looking furniture in the city's expensive boutiques. But what he'd discovered, when he finally mustered up the courage to enter those shops, was that the pieces themselves were not as well constructed as they could be.

"I know I can make better furniture," he said, and then caught himself. "I mean, not to brag."

When it was April's turn to tell her story, she felt self-conscious. She wasn't expecting to feel so outclassed by this farm boy. She'd thought that all Amish people did was sit around singing hymns and darning socks. What was she supposed to say in response? Hers wasn't exactly an inspirational story about starting an organic cheese business in order to finance a luxury furniture line. Should she tell him that she was in a court-ordered NA program at the moment, and that she'd started using when she was twelve? Should she tell him how close she was to doing prison time? This Joseph was a strange combination of ambitious and naive—April was neither. But, inspired by him for a moment, she decided to go for it.

"Well," she said, "my dream is to play in a band."

April had never told anyone this. She'd hardly ever even admitted it to herself. But, now, there it was, out there. She'd revealed her deepest, most vulnerable self to this total stranger. She glanced over at Joseph, to see what he made of this confession and found him looking at her inquisitively.

"You know . . . to play music. Sing, play guitar. Travel all around. Rock out."

Joseph turned away from her, and stared ahead, sitting perfectly still, a shadow over his face, lost in thought. April suddenly lost all her confidence.

"I mean, whatever, right?" she added quickly. "I know I'm just working at a bakery right now. But like, one day, I mean. I know it's hokey."

Joseph stayed silent for a moment longer than April could tolerate. And she began to reach for her phone, looking for some escape from what was becoming a rather embarrassing interaction. But then Joseph spoke.

"I really like music," he said.

This comment was one of the most generic things anyone had ever said to April and yet, it made her heart jump.

"*Really?*" she said, overexcitedly. "What kind?"

"Oh," Joseph replied, "I don't know much about it. We don't listen to it, you know. But we sing in church and I really like that. It's my favorite time of the week."

"Something special happens when people sing together," April said.

Joseph turned and looked at her, as though noticing her for the first time, and said, "That's true." Their eyes met for a powerful second; then they both looked away abruptly, and in a way that only confirmed the power of the gaze.

April, trying to dispel the awkwardness, spoke quickly.

"What's your favorite song?" she asked.

Joseph became quiet and deeply contemplative. April giggled.

"I mean, don't give it *too* much thought . . ." she said. She was beginning to become accustomed to, and amused by, his long, serious silences.

April looked at him slyly. He seemed to be struggling with something.

"Well," he finally said, "I heard this song once," he began. And then stopped, apparently unsure of himself.

"Tell me about it," April urged him.

He'd heard the song once, when he was in a Home Depot, accompanying one of his non-Amish employers on a supplies run. The moment Joseph heard the song, he loved it. But because he didn't own a device that would replay the song, he'd never heard it again. And anyway, he wouldn't know what song it was, even if he did find himself near a device.

"*Really?*" April asked. "You never heard the song again."

"No," replied Joseph.

"You heard it only once?"

"Yes."

"And when was that?"

"Oh, about two years ago."

"Wow," April said, and then got very quiet, trying to imagine what that was like: to love a song and never hear it again. And to be okay with living with such restrictions.

"What was it, the song? What was it called?"

"I don't know," Joseph said.

April could feel herself growing agitated.

"Oh, c'mon! Do you remember any of the words?"

"It was about a woman from Louisiana and a man from Mississippi. Or maybe a man from Louisiana and a woman from Mississippi? I don't remember. But it was a real fun song."

April reached for her phone.

"Is it okay if I use the phone for you?" she asked, holding it up.

Joseph laughed.

"Sure," he said. "Wouldn't be the first time."

April began typing.

"Got it!"

She showed him search results for an old country song, "Louisiana Woman, Mississippi Man." There was a link to a video. Joseph held his face far from it, as though he were contemplating a beautiful but dangerous insect. April giggled.

"Wanna hear it? I can play it right now."

Joseph shifted in his seat.

"Oh," he said. "I wouldn't want to put you out."

"Omigod, don't be silly!" April said. "Lemme play it for you . . . if that's, like, okay."

"It's okay," Joseph said.

April clicked on the video. She put the phone close to his ear and she leaned in. For the next two minutes, they listened to Conway Twitty and Loretta Lynn singing a flirty, twangy duet over a sexy slide guitar about how nothing, not even the big river, can keep a Louisiana woman away from her Mississippi man.

Being so close to him, April could sense just how large and strong his body was. Their heads were only inches apart.

April and Joseph's eyes met and lingered comfortably for a heart-pounding two seconds. Nothing else in the world existed except that gaze.

And then, a long silence. It was not an uncomfortable silence at all. But the opposite: an intimate stillness, similar, in fact, to the quietness shared by people who have just finished singing a harmony, who sit together listening to the strong but fading chords settling in their ears. It was a pleasant, satisfying, shared stillness. They smiled at each other.

April suddenly became aware of the darkness that surrounded them inside the bus, where all the passengers were now asleep. She became aware of the darkness outside that surrounded the bus as it glided through the midnight cornfields. She let her breath blend into the humming tread of tires against pavement.

The gaze that they had shared had been more than a gaze: it was a very real and physical *exchange*. An agreement. April had given something of herself to Joseph, and Joseph had given something of himself to April. She wasn't sure, exactly, what he'd given her. But she felt it, the small heft of it, like the weight of a sleeping thing, resting in her hands. And now, in the silence, she cradled it tightly.

A surge of emotion rose in April, and with it, the ardent hope that he would take her by the hand. Instead, she just looked at his hand, which was gently squeezing the armrest only an inch away from her. It was such a strong hand. And an eloquent one. The thickness of his hand spoke of constructive labor.

He was so quiet, she wondered if he was asleep. But he wasn't. She could tell because his hand continued to squeeze the armrest, an inch from her— ever so gently, or at least, as gentle as such a strong hand could be. She shifted her leg as many centimeters closer to his hand as she could without touching him. Close enough for the rocking of the bus to bring his hand and her leg into regular intervals of gentle contact.

She closed her eyes and pretended to sleep. As she fell asleep for real, she felt her leg finally lose its ability to resist his hand. It met his touch for a long, warm two seconds. In her last waking thought,

April reckoned this contact was one second beyond what might be called an "accidental touch." He was keeping his hand there on purpose. Finally, Joseph removed his hand from the armrest, and as she fell into slumber, she tried to suppress a smile.

Chapter Three

Rose looked at the concrete wall. She dragged herself up to it and put her palm against it. It was ice-cold. But it offered relief. She was, she suddenly realized, drenched in sweat, her head swimming against riptides of fever. Now she found herself leaning her body against the wall; now she found herself pressing her cheek against it, absorbing the soothing coldness of it. Her movements didn't seem like decisions. Her body was just reacting. But slowly. And her brain was moving even slower, registering these actions with a second or two delay. It must have been only a few seconds, but it was enough to deeply disorient her. Maybe it wasn't a one-second delay? Maybe it was one minute? Maybe a day? A week. Maybe a month had passed.

Her feet were somehow moving now, shuffling. Were they shackled? It felt like they were. She turned to look, and a sharp pain gripped her neck. But there were no chains or ropes of any kind on her feet. She arrived at the edge of the wall. At a corner. She now realized she was running her hand over the corner, sticking her fingers into the nook where concrete met concrete, as though looking for something stuck inside it. Her fingers seemed to want to confirm that the world was still three-dimensional, and that the time was now, the present.

The cold reality of the concrete wall might have confirmed the existence of space and time, but it didn't tell her who she was. The memories in her mind of a past life were not even images but sounds—a melody of a song, the tone of a woman's voice. They were as vague and paper-thin as the suddenly recalled sounds of a long-forgotten dream. She now found her brain telling her that this wall was where she'd always been, always lived. This was all there was. Her eye caught the image of a tattoo, a rose snaking around her arm. She saw it. She looked at it. But it didn't register in her brain, didn't connect to anything, and it immediately slipped out of mind and was forgotten.

Rose slumped against the wall. She was sinking. She balled herself up on the ground, back against the wall, holding her knees to her chest. All of a sudden she was intensely cold. So, so cold. She could not move anything. There was nothing near her, or anywhere, that could give warmth. And even if there was, she couldn't move any part of her body to get closer to it.

This was what it meant to freeze to death. It meant being a frozen planet in empty expanses of space. In a death that creeps as slow as ice, the brain and the organs are the last things to go. Rose felt it unmistakably. Because water expands as it freezes, the body, which is mostly water, expands internally, pushing slowly but with increasing firmness against its own veins and arteries. Pressing on the heart and lungs. Pressing against the brain. The brain starts to shock and malfunction. But slowly. The organs continue working, though with painful inefficiency, with occasional spasms that wake the victim up, just as they begin to drift off into the relief of unconsciousness, as though to prolong the agony of witnessing, utterly alone, from deep within a hardening body, living death. Rose was too exhausted to scream. But her head resounded with a long, hopeless, radiating shriek.

April arrived at Reading Market fifteen minutes early, rather than her customary fifteen-to-thirty minutes late.

"Hey there," Carmen said, as April walked into the bakery, "you're in early today."

Carmen paused in the midst of entering yesterday's cash register numbers into her iPad; she watched April make a beeline for an apron that hung on a rack near the counter, then pull up her sleeves, tie back her hair, wash her hands, and get immediately to work transferring fresh-made croissants from a baking rack to a display shelf.

"Look at you," Carmen continued. Then Carmen took her own advice and took a closer look at April.

"Wait, there's something different about you," she said.

April just shrugged and continued stacking croissants.

"What is it?" Carmen said, squinting at April. "Hey . . . you're wearing extra makeup!" Carmen noted.

"Are you gonna do this all day?"

"Okay, and now you're *blushing!*" Carmen got up from her seat and walked toward April. "So let's see here," she said, and stood right in front of April, trying to look her directly in the eye. "You're *early*. You're wearing *purple* eye shadow. And now . . . you're blushing? *What* is going on, girl?"

April told her about the bus ride. About Joseph. About listening to the song with him, just the two of them, in the dark bus, leaning in with their heads close together, listening to those two old-timey country people singing about how the Mississippi River couldn't keep them apart. And she told Carmen about how strong Joseph's hands were.

"His hands, huh?" Carmen said, narrowing her eyes. "Hmm."

April just smiled.

"And this kid works here, at Reading?"

"Yeah! He was the guy who was posting the 'Missing' signs for Rose. He works at the Amish diner," April said, pointing across the way. "But only half the week. And not on Sundays, because that's the Lord's Day."

"Oh boy," Carmen said. And then she added, "Well, you look really nice, sweetie."

* * *

For the next few days, April arrived earlier than she ever had. And she showed up wearing her best outfits. During any lulls, she'd wander over to the Amish diner and wave to Joseph as he worked. She'd watch him closely. When he took breaks, she took breaks. They ate lunch together. She brought him cookies from the bakery. She even convinced him to join her on the other side of the market, far from prying eyes.

Since April was actually working harder than usual, Carmen couldn't really complain but, still, something about this flirtation bothered her. When she saw April lingering near the diner, she'd call her over and make up a task for her to do. When she caught April messing up a customer's change—because she was spying on the Amish diner—Carmen came up behind her and whispered, "Stay on point, hon."

Once, she was even more direct. When April arrived at work looking particularly stylish, Carmen greeted her by saying, "It's not like he's gonna notice—and even if he does, those people don't go for that." But she immediately regretted saying it when she saw April's face drop.

She tried to rein in her comments after that. But as they mopped up the bakery one evening, shortly before closing time, Carmen couldn't help herself.

"Have you spoken to Sergeant Connors recently?" she said.

"About what?" April replied, distractedly, as she piled the chairs on top of the tables.

"Really, April?" Carmen said, folding her arms. "About what? About your sister, who's been missing for more than a month now."

April threw down the rag she was holding. She put her hand on her hip and glared. Carmen pretended not to be intimidated. Even though Carmen was playing the role of mentor, she was still terrified of April's fury, her street toughness.

"What is your problem, Carmen?"

"I just want what's best for you," Carmen said, almost inaudibly.

"You're *not* my mother."

"Neither is your mother."

April's boldness drained away completely. She hadn't expected the sharp retort—with its bite of betrayal, since she'd only recently, and with trepidation, shared certain facts about her family background with Carmen.

"Oh honey," Carmen said, "I'm so sorry. I didn't mean to throw that back at you like that. Look, I'm just worried about you. Joseph seems like a good kid, probably. I just don't want you to get hurt now, with everything that's going on. And also, seriously, you need to talk to Sergeant Connors."

April's fury returned, spinning slightly out of her control. She stared at Carmen with eyes filling with tears, her lip trembling just a bit. April seemed to be holding her head up *at* Carmen, defiantly—but the quivering gave her away.

"Is that all?" April said. "We done here?"

Carmen nodded, and April was out the door.

But Carmen and April soon made up. This dynamic, of fighting and making up, and, in the process, creating an even tighter bond, made April miss her sister even more. She channeled her longing for Rose into her growing Joseph fixation. They were seeing much more of each other, and their gifts were becoming more personal. She would do research for him about the cheese and furniture industries and bring him large piles of carefully organized printouts on these subjects. He would make her little gifts out of wood.

Even though she was on good terms with Carmen, she still wasted no opportunity to get away from the bakery, to give herself some space. Her breaks from work were getting longer by the day. When a summer heatwave broke, and a mild spring-like spell cast itself over the city, April persuaded Joseph to go for longer and longer walks. In her mind, April believed that the farther she could take Joseph from Reading Terminal Market—the more distance she could put between the two of them and the disapproving glances of Joseph's Amish cousins and Carmen, too—the more Joseph belonged to her alone. And the more time she spent with him, the more distance she could get from her anxieties about Rose.

She and Joseph were never truly alone, though. As they walked through the streets of downtown Philadelphia, people would stop and stare at them. From the faces of these strangers, their giggles, their secretive photos, it was obvious what everyone was thinking: what was this hip young woman doing walking around with an Amish guy? City people, used to seeing everything, hadn't, however seen *this*.

On a walk down a picture-perfect stretch of Delancey Street, lined by magnolias, April took Joseph's hand. They walked almost an entire block hand in hand. The feeling of his strong hand thrilled April. The attention of passersby didn't bother her in the least. On the contrary, she liked it. A lot. People seemed not only amused by this unlikely couple but, in many cases, charmed. The sight of April and Joseph put a smile on people's faces. April wasn't used to pleasing people—it felt strange but not unpleasant.

But it was obvious, too, that Joseph was having the exact opposite experience. He was uncomfortable from the moment she'd taken his hand into hers. And she could tell that his discomfort was only growing with each smiling passerby. After a few minutes, she released his hand, with a sigh. She could tell that Joseph felt much more at ease. And this made her sigh again. She didn't try to touch him again—and they didn't speak of it.

* * *

Joseph was the youngest of seven children. Like many large families, the siblings of the Young family divided themselves into two or three separate groups. In his family, the division went like this: the four elder brothers were one unit; the second unit consisted of two sisters and little Joseph. The Young family took birth order very seriously. The oldest children, especially the boys, were given greater responsibility—and they were also given the lion's share of the family's resources.

Once Joseph's older brothers were married off, according to their birth order, the family put all its energies into helping them, and their young brides, locate, purchase, and begin to cultivate farmland nearby. After all these exertions, and after working to secure marriages for their daughters, too, while also maintaining their own family farm, the Youngs had little remaining capital—and even less energy— to help Joseph find his way.

This situation left Joseph with fewer prospects than his siblings—but it also gave him an unusual degree of freedom. From a very early age, he was schooled in the Amish ways, but, at the same time, he was subtly encouraged to be more independent than his siblings. This small seed of independence was something that he grew to cherish. It became a part of who he was—perhaps too much so for his family's comfort.

"Your boy's got some serious *rumspringa* eyes," Carmen said to April, one early afternoon at the bakery. The lunch crowd had passed through, and the two women had a moment to linger at the counter and catch their breath. Carmen, of late, had been trying to be more supportive of Joseph.

"What's a rum stinger?" April said. "Sounds like a cocktail."

Carmen laughed.

"Rum*springa,*" she said. "In their language, it means 'running around.' It's basically this period of time that could last from the late teens 'til the early twenties, when Amish kids are allowed to bend the rules a little. The idea is to let them have a bit more of an outlet to be teens—but at the same time to bring the boys and girls together to let them meet and match up for marriages. But some of them really break out. I think your boy Joseph is one of those."

"Really?" April said brightly. "What makes you think so?"

Carmen grinned.

"*What?*" April said, blushing.

"Oh nothing. Just never seen you look so interested in anything I've ever said. Like, ever."

"Just shut up and tell me more about rum stinkers!"

"Well, let's start with that business idea he has . . . to make fancy furniture? That's not a very Amish thing to do. These people don't make or sell luxury items. It's against everything they believe in. And when I heard him talking about it to you, I thought,

'Oh boy, this kid is going to get himself in *trouble*.' And then, of course, there's how he talks to you. Well, first of all, *that* he talks to you. But mostly, *how* he talks to you. . . ."

"How does he talk to me?" April was almost nose to nose now with Carmen.

"Oh, come on, April. You know exactly how."

The next day, when April was sitting next to Joseph on a bench in a park, gazing into his dark green eyes, she decided it was time to ask the big question.

"Are you allowed to date girls outside of your community? Asking for a friend."

"No," he said, turning away.

"That's it," April replied. "Just . . . *no?* And what happens if you do?"

"You don't," he said. "If you do, you are out. Sometimes someone from outside joins. But that is rare."

"How do you feel about that?"

"I understand it," he said. "It's how things need to be."

"You're okay with it?"

"It doesn't matter if I'm okay with it," Joseph said. "It's just how it is."

April couldn't detect from his tone what Joseph really meant. At these moments, when some barrier came up, it always seemed Joseph became particularly difficult to read. Just when she needed clarity, he'd speak in riddles.

"Okay . . ." April said, trying to process Joseph's words. "But what about *rumspringers?*"

Joseph smiled and seemed to loosen up a bit.

"*Rumspringa,*" he corrected her.

"Yeah, that. *Rumspringa.*"

"It doesn't mean what you think it means."

"How do you know what I think it means?"

"I live in the world," Joseph said.

"Well, yeah, but like in a different world . . ."

"No," Joseph said, turning to April. "Same world. Just a different way of living in it."

They sat quietly for a moment.

"Does your family approve of your idea, the fancy furniture business thing?"

"They don't understand it," he replied. "And those that do, don't like it. It's not what we do."

"Do they want you to do something else?"

"Well, no. There's not as much farmland in Pennsylvania as there used to be. Even my brothers had to look for plots in Iowa and Wisconsin. A lot of people do nowadays. And anyway, my family doesn't have money to buy anything right now. They need me to find something else."

"So they don't like the furniture idea but they'll support it."

"If it lets me get settled and get married, they won't object."

"Get married . . . to an Amish girl, you mean?"

"Of course," Joseph said.

* * *

The next day, during the short break after lunchtime, April pulled off her apron, tossed it onto a hook, and, without thinking, began to walk toward the Amish diner, toward Joseph. It was their unofficial meeting time. Then she stopped in her tracks. *What am I* doing? she thought. *He's just going to disappear one day. He's just slumming it with me.*

April noticed Carmen looking at her from behind the counter. It was obvious that Carmen could tell exactly what she was thinking, and it only deepened April's irritation. Determined not to give Carmen the pleasure of being right, April turned around and continued toward the Amish diner with renewed resolve—but she didn't stop there. As she passed the diner, April made a special effort not to look for Joseph. No. Let him see her walk by, ignoring him.

So what if Joseph wasn't serious about her? Was she serious about him? This farmer boy was looking to get *married*, literally the last thing on earth April wanted to do now. And yeah, seven babies? No, thanks. April wasn't about to play farmer's wife. She laughed to herself at the thought of walking around, demurely wearing a prairie dress and singing hymns.

As April walked out into the open air, into the warm spring day, she flung off her flannel shirt, tied it around her waist, and stretched in her tank top, enjoying the sun warming her bare arms and neck. If Joseph were around, she'd probably keep the flannel on, so as not to scandalize his Amish sensibilities too much.

Forget him, she thought. And walked through the streets, careful to avoid the spots she associated with Joseph.

April had plenty of other things to worry about it. Joseph, after all, wasn't an actual problem—he was, in fact, the distraction from her problems. Joseph was the easy part of her life. That, at least, was the hope.

In the meantime, the hard parts of April's life seemed to be getting harder by the day. She still owed money all over town. At war with at least two ex-boyfriends, she was constantly watching her back for dangerous interactions. There were entire neighborhoods in Philly that April wouldn't set foot in, for fear of running into potentially hazardous encounters, people who triggered her, people who, if she even saw them, much less talked to them, would lead her down a road that would quickly land her in jail.

The reason she was penniless when she'd first arrived that day at Carmen's bakery was that she'd just quit a job in Fishtown, in North Philly, for fear of running into her (most recent) abusive ex. And because of that fear, she'd lost a shot at work. There were just too many traps set for her around town.

And jobs didn't come easy. She couldn't seem to hold down work. Inevitably her boss would reveal himself—it was almost always some man—to be a jerk, or worse. Eventually April would tell him so and she'd be out of a job. Now that she was working at the bakery, she had some cash flow but, if history were any guide, it would be temporary.

And what kind of support system did she really have? If Joseph suffered from too much family, April had the opposite problem: barely any. April's father died when she was twelve. Her mother was a broken-down alcoholic, who spent her days inserting coins into slot machines in Atlantic City. Her mother lived with an abusive boyfriend who, more than once, had aggressively tried to kiss April. The final straw had come when her mother had found Rose's checkbook and forged a check to herself from it. Neither sister trusted their mother and they avoided contact with her. The sudden recent disappearance of her sister was not only a painful and unsettling development, but also a major blow to April's social world. She simply didn't have much else.

Well, she had Carmen now. And, it seemed, things were going well on that front. But she was just waiting for the other shoe to drop, waiting for Carmen to lose patience with her, get angry at her, ask her to leave the bakery. She was doing everything in her power to make it work, but she knew the patterns of her life; somehow everything got fouled up in the end. She would survive, yes, but she would lose everything in the process.

And then there was Joseph. He was supposed to be the easy part of her day. But the more she told herself that, the more it seemed like a line. Was he really a part of her life? What did he even know about her? And if he ever were to know, would he talk to her anymore? April's constant thoughts about Joseph were beginning to become yet another problem. It seemed that the only way out of thinking about Joseph was to spend more time with him. But that, of course, just sounded like another trap.

The situation with Rose was so bad that April could barely even get her mind around it anymore. She'd been checking in with Sergeant Connors every few days. Then it became every week. Then even less frequently. She couldn't take the constant bad news, the blank looks of the cops. She hated lying to them by withholding everything she knew about Ricky, and she feared that these lies would catch up with her.

Ricky had never contacted her after she'd barged into his shop that day. She contemplated going back—but had put it off. At first, it was a calculated move. She wanted to see how he'd respond to her note. Then, after his silence, she realized she'd lost her confidence. She began to suspect that a second visit would be, at best, unproductive. And at worse, dangerous. So she'd waited. And when nothing happened, when there was no news of any kind, she began to panic, to lose sleep.

Then something clicked in her. Her panic was replaced by something even more powerful: denial. Admitting that this was happening had simply become too dangerous. Of all the bad things that had beset April in her life, the disappearance of literally the only person she trusted and loved was something she lacked the language to describe. It was something beyond fear or anxiety or even extreme sadness. It was something that, if she looked at it honestly, would force her to question her own existence, her identity. What happened to a person when the one constant in their life, the thing that sustained them, was suddenly gone, vanished, as if it never existed? What happened, April believed, was that you also ceased to exist. For the sake of her sanity, out of some primal instinct for basic survival, she simply couldn't think about it. Not anymore.

She found her brain telling her, *She'll probably call any minute, she'll show up, she's fine.* It was just impossible to imagine that something had really happened to Rose. This kind of thing didn't really happen. This wasn't some movie.

There were moments of hard clarity, when April realized that being passive, allowing denial to set in, was reckless. Her new sobriety gave her these moments of clarity, and so she grew to despise her sobriety. But as long as she was sober, her brain could do the math. Every day and week that passed, every minute really, meant worse odds of finding Rose. Time was not on her side. But just as quickly as April had these thoughts, she let them go. There were professional detectives on the case. What could she really do anyway? How did endlessly worrying really help?

When April returned from her walk, Reading Market was mostly quiet. She walked past the Amish diner and, in her peripheral vision, she noticed Joseph at the register. She saw that he was looking at her, but she ignored him and walked on. Without a word, she arrived back in the bakery, slipped into her apron and rubber gloves, grabbed her trusty dough scraper, and picked up where she'd left off: cutting sharp triangles out of a giant slab of raspberry-dotted dough, shaping and smoothing them with the side of the dough scraper, weighing the triangles to ensure uniformity of size (1.5 ounces each), and setting each on a tray, ready to be baked into tomorrow's scones. When she got going, it felt like a comforting and increasingly familiar rhythm, and she could work placidly like that for hours.

Whitey sat at his desk, looking at his dead cell phone. He'd mostly stopped picking up the phone. He would give it some use every day, for a few minutes, so as not to raise any suspicions, not tip off anyone who might be listening. But in reality, he now kept the phone only for emergencies. Ever since he'd had that little scare: when he began to suspect that he might have an enemy inside the FBI, in addition to the well-placed friends he'd cultivated.

He'd been warned by his guys that the phone was now too dangerous to use for anything related to business. Well, actually, one of his guys said it was too dangerous ("How you ever gonna really know who's watching?") and another had said it was fine. ("If the cops can secure their devices, so can we.") Whitey went with the cautious advice. And not only that, he put the other guy, the one who'd told him to keep using the phone, on notice. Why was that guy telling him to risk it? Was he trying to get Whitey in trouble? Was that guy a snitch? Whitey decided to keep an eye on him. Eventually he would test him. And if he failed the test, the guy would have to be gotten rid of.

Whitey was sick of this game. Sick of cat and mouse. He was just a businessman. He helped people. The people who worked for him loved him. He gave back to the community, far more than most people. Many regarded him as a kind of legend. He should have been celebrated by the public. Instead he was treated like a criminal. At this point in his life, he had given up on being appreciated. He just wanted to be left alone.

He was happier without his phone. It was a relief. He liked getting his messages in person. Liked to look into the eyes of the person who was talking to him, liked to size up the person, to detect what they weren't telling him. You couldn't do that by text. And Whitey was good at it.

There was a knock. Whitey's hand slowly and calmly went to his gun, as was his practice.

"Yeah," he shouted.

One of his guys peeked in from behind the door.

"Uh . . . sir," he said. The word *sir* sounded clumsy in his mouth, and Whitey winced a bit.

"Come in all the way," Whitey said, with an edge of annoyance. "Let me see you."

How many times did Whitey have to instruct his men how to enter a room with him? How many times did he have to repeat himself? Whitey looked at his man. He was fidgety and distracted. But then again, the guy was always like that. Whitey understood his world. He understood that if you wanted helpers who were capable of violence it was unlikely that they'd also be well-mannered and of even temperament. That was just the sad reality of it. And, anyway, when one of his men was too cultivated, that worried him even more.

"What is it?" Whitey said.

"Uh, that guy Ricky's here to see you," he said. "Says he has a meeting with you."

"About?" Whitey said, wearily.

"Some girl, I guess," the guy said. "Says he needs a favor."

Whitey closed his eyes and sighed.

"Send him in."

Chapter Four

Carmen was beginning to trust April with more tasks around the bakery. Even though she was still having some trouble arriving on time, April was a hard worker, and smart. When she tried, she could even be friendly with customers and a good saleswoman. She had come up with some clever marketing ideas (*"On your birthday come into Metropolitan Bakery for a FREE brownie with a candle on top!"*), and had created a large and devoted Instagram following for the bakery. Carmen was watching April carefully, and was continually impressed by her. It wasn't long before she entrusted April with the keys to close up shop.

On Tuesdays and Thursdays, April would close, then head straight to her NA meeting, where she received a hero's welcome for showing up with two bagfuls of delicious treats, leftovers from her day at Metropolitan Bakery.

On one of these Thursdays, just as April was tying up the last garbage bag and getting ready to run to her meeting, she felt someone looking at her. She turned around.

"How do you know where I work?" she said.

"You're not the only one who snoops around," Ricky said, leaning against the door that separated the kitchen from the front counter, blocking April in.

He was dressed in cargo jeans, a tan work jacket, roofer's boots, and a Phillies cap. It was as if he hadn't changed his clothes since the last time she'd seen him, more than six months earlier.

"So you got my message."

"Yeah," he said, crossing his arms. "Didn't like your tone, though."

"Did I hurt your feelings?" April said.

She quickly glanced at the knife rack that hung next to the big oven. Ricky's eyes followed hers there. He grinned slyly.

"I don't know where Rose is," he said.

April just stared at him.

"I'm sure she's fine," he said. "You know how she is."

April continued staring.

"I don't know where she is, April," he said. "Why would I?"

"*Why would you* . . . Seriously? How about this: Why would *I* trust *you*? 'Cause I think we both know why I don't. So why don't you stop pretending?"

"That tone, again," Ricky said. "Very rude. Can't we just talk?"

"My sister is missing. And you seem supercalm about it. Doesn't exactly make me trust you."

"I don't need you to trust me."

"Why are you here, Ricky?"

"You said you wanted to talk."

"Where is my sister?"

"No idea."

"That's funny; you always seem so full of ideas."

"I got nothing to do with this."

"With *what,* Ricky? What do you got nothing to do with?"

"Have you talked to the cops?"

"Why do you care, since you got nothing to do with it?"

Ricky stiffened. April quickly decided to change her tack.

"I haven't talked to anyone," she lied. "But I'm gonna find my sister. And if I need the cops to help me, then yeah, I'm gonna talk to them. Give me one reason I shouldn't."

"Since when did you get so hard?" he said, with a laugh.

"When was the last time you saw Rose?"

"Nice place here. Can I have a cookie?"

"When was the last time you saw my sister?"

"Not sure, maybe a month ago."

"Ricky, think about it for real: what day was it, what time was it? What did she tell you? Say what you know."

Ricky stretched, revealing a gun tucked into his belt. He noticed April notice it.

"Oh, you like this bad boy?" he said, pulling the gun out. "A Glock 19. Great piece of hardware." He took aim at the oven. He seemed freer, more friendly even, with a gun in his hand. April jumped at the opportunity.

"When did you last see Rose?" she said. "Tell me the date and time."

Ricky rolled his eyes.

"It was at the shop, after dark," he said. "Must have been a Monday or Tuesday. 'Cause those are the only days I go in now. She came by to pick some stuff up. It was right before her birthday, because I remember she got pissy with me about that."

"What was the last thing she said to you?"

"The last thing?" Ricky said. He seemed to be genuinely trying to remember. "I think it was basically *G'bye, never wanna see your dumb face again*."

"And did she tell you where she was going?"

"Nope."

"How was she traveling?"

"Car."

"She doesn't have a car."

"I think someone was waiting for her outside the shop."

"Who? Did you see the car?"

"No idea who, and didn't see the car."

"That was the last time you spoke?"

"Yeah. After that I didn't hear from her. We weren't talking much by then anyway."

"Did you try to talk to her?"

"Yeah, I sent her a text or two."

"Can I see?"

"See what?"

"The texts. Show them to me."

"How about *no?*"

"Show me. Unless you're hiding something."

"I'm done here."

Ricky glanced around quickly, and he looked up to see if there was a camera in the space—there was not. When he suddenly noticed that he was still holding the Glock, he laughed to himself, as though delighted by his good fortune. Without saying another word, he used the butt of the pistol to smash an oversized glass container, full of whole wheat flour, one of four antique jars that Carmen used to hold supplies. Then he methodically shattered the remaining three containers, smiling with satisfaction as the cracks widened and immediately gave way to four rushing cascades of flour. April wanted to cry out, but she held back, with great effort, not wanting to give him any further satisfaction. For a moment, they both watched quietly as a giant pile of broken glass and flour rose suddenly on the floor.

When he was done, Ricky lifted his gun and pointed it directly at April's face. She held her breath. He stared at her with vacant dead eyes.

"Don't tell the cops anything stupid, April," he said, wearily. "Just don't get mixed up in this, okay? I know you're stressed about Rose. But don't be stupid. And don't show up at Nick's again."

April missed the NA meeting that night. But it wasn't for lack of effort. After Ricky left, she'd immediately locked up the bakery and run to the bus. She left the giant mess Ricky had made, planning to return to the bakery after the meeting to clean up. She didn't want Carmen to walk into that disaster scene first thing in the morning.

She'd waited for fifteen minutes at the bus stop, until she decided to splurge and take an Uber, only to realize she'd left her phone at the bakery. By the time she arrived at the church across town, the NA meeting was over. In order to avoid a penalty from the court, she would have to get an excuse letter from her boss. But what would April tell Carmen?

When April arrived back at Reading Terminal Market that night, at almost 11:00 P.M., the front door to the market was locked. And her key to the bakery didn't open that lock. There was nothing to be done about it. April would not be able to clean the mess before Carmen arrived the next morning. And when Carmen did show up, she would find a scene of destruction. She would find four large expensive antique containers, which she loved, and an entire day's worth of flour, ruined. She would find the mess on the floor, as though April had carelessly left it there without dealing with it. April would have a lot of explaining to do.

April would be there first thing in the morning, to tell Carmen what had happened. But that explanation, of course, wouldn't calm Carmen's nerves. On the contrary. April would have to admit that the damage was inflicted *intentionally* by Rose's vindictive ex, the kind of guy who could and possibly did harm Rose.

And when Carmen asked, *So how does this gangster know you work at my bakery?*

April would have to say, *No idea.*

And why did he smash everything up?

April would say, *Because he was upset about the questions I asked about Rose's disappearance. And he didn't like that I'm talking to the cops.*

There was no way to spin this story, no way to make it sound less threatening than it was. Well, maybe one way: April could omit the detail about the gun.

Carmen would be understandably angry. Even if she tried to forgive, she would feel betrayed and violated and just plain terrified. She would certainly demand even more contact with the police. But what would April, the sole witness, actually *say* in this police report? Would she explain why Ricky was there? There was no way around it. If she was going to file a report about Ricky's damage, she might incur the wrath of Ricky; and if they didn't report it, well, that would make Carmen feel unprotected and anxious. The trust that April had won from Carmen had vanished in an instant.

And still, despite all of these complications, all of the upset and anger that would descend on her tomorrow morning, April had other things on her mind. As she waited for the bus to take her back to her apartment in South Philly, she felt almost delirious with excitement. She had a bunch of new clues about her sister's disappearance. Ricky hadn't stopped by to make a social call—he was nervous. And his nerves incriminated him. April was on the right trail. She was certain of it.

When she finally arrived home that night, she ran to her kitchen table and, without even bothering to take off her coat, sat down and began scribbling all the details of what had happened that night, leaving nothing out. Anything could be a clue.

Ten tense minutes into the meeting, Whitey looked at his watch.

"This is the second time you've come to me this month," he said to Ricky. "And it's the last time we meet. I'm a busy man. I think you know that."

"I know," Ricky said. "I'm busy, too."

Whitey couldn't help himself; he laughed. He loved when fools showed their cards to him. It made things so much easier that way. And it was not unamusing to watch them in their sad effort to bluff like tough guys.

"Well, okay," Whitey said. "We're both busy, so why don't you leave now?"

Whitey began to shuffle some papers on his desk and turned his attention elsewhere. He tried to contain his smile, as he sensed Ricky, who hadn't budged in his chair, begin fidgeting awkwardly. Whitey held him there like that, in silent torture, for a long minute. Finally, Ricky could take it no longer.

"Well, there is one thing."

"Let me guess."

"The girl," said Ricky.

"Of course," replied Whitey. "Isn't that the reason you're really here? You've created quite a mess for yourself."

Whitey leaned back in his chair and indulged himself in a long look at Ricky. He enjoyed watching Ricky try, and fail, to control his anger.

"That's one way of looking at it," Ricky said. "I went to speak to the sister."

"I don't care. And I don't want to hear about it."

Ricky seethed.

"There's nothing I can do to help you," Whitey said. "Which I think you know."

"I can pay."

Whitey was no longer amused.

"Do not lie to me," Whitey said.

"I can come up with the money."

"This is not about money."

"I'm not lying to you."

"You need to *go!*" Whitey shouted. "*Now.*"

He leaned over the desk and put his face inches from Ricky's, breathing hard.

"Go," Whitey whispered through clenched teeth.

Ricky didn't move. It wasn't defiance that kept him. His legs were paralyzed. Whitey said nothing more but stared directly into his eyes, from inches away. A pall of cold fear gripped Ricky. Whitey's gaze was like that of a predatory animal. There was nothing in his eyes that Ricky could recognize as human or sympathetic. These were the eyes of someone who had killed in cold blood. It was known that Whitey didn't just order deaths; he went out of his way to participate in the dirty work of slaughter. It was unwise of him to do that—and yet he got his hands dirty simply because murder was something he enjoyed. Ricky knew about it. Now he saw that hunger for himself. With a slight panic rising in his lower back, he weakly mustered his legs to move. He stood up and walked out slowly, careful not to turn his back on the predator whose gaze remained fixed upon him.

As Ricky retreated, he could hear Whitey muttering, "This is the last time we meet."

For the next week, April felt uptight. It seemed as if everyone was watching her. After the Ricky incident, Carmen wouldn't let her out of her sight.

Joseph, of course, was also watching her, for other reasons.

And Joseph's cousins, the ones who ran the Amish diner, were growing more suspicious of Joseph and April's relationship. At least, it seemed that way to April. She saw their looks, the way they carefully watched him as he cut out for breaks. She saw the glances they exchanged. And she saw, especially, how their suspicion was making Joseph himself feel uncomfortable around April. Sometimes he would just shake his head and continue working when April came around the diner, almost ignoring her. And even when he did take a break and went on a walk with her, he seemed more distant, more distracted.

One afternoon when April wandered over to the Amish diner, Joseph seemed more tense than she'd ever seen him.

"It's not a good time," he said, and turned around to walk away. April gently grasped his wrist, but he slipped out of her hold and looked around to see if anyone had seen this gesture.

"April," he said, "you really shouldn't."

"I'm sorry," she said. "But also . . . not sorry."

They just stood there, looking at each other for a long moment. April could sense that something else was wrong.

"What's the matter?" she said.

"We're having a tough day over here," Joseph said. One of his aunts, who worked in the diner, had suddenly gotten very ill. And, on top of that, his aunt was the one who usually handled orders and deliveries. In her sudden absence, the diner had failed to order a large shipment of bread that they needed for a catering job that evening. Everyone was scrambling and nervous.

"I got this," April said.

Before Joseph could reply, April marched up to Joseph's uncle. She had watched this man from afar, with curiosity and fear: he looked like every old-time bearded American president rolled into one large frame, with a Mt. Rushmore-sized forehead deeply etched with worry wrinkles. He was the boss of the diner and was not, in April's experience, much given to smiling. In her mind, she referred to him as Ebenezer. His actual name, it turned out, was Levi. April hadn't ever exchanged a word with him— at worst, she was the recipient of his disapproving looks; at best, his neutral gaze. But now she was marching up to the cash register, where he was standing.

"Hey," she said. "Uh, I mean, hello. I hear you have a bread problem."

April watched as the man's deep forehead wrinkles somehow deepened even further. But other than that, his expression did not change at all. Nor did he say a word. Instead he just slowly turned his gaze past April's shoulder, to where Joseph was standing. April turned around just in time to see Joseph nod slightly and look down. She turned back to Ebenezer/Levi and saw him squint ever so slightly. She had the sudden impulse to turn around and run.

"Look, I'm not trying to cause any trouble here," April said, "but I can help you. I work over there," she said, pointing toward the Metropolitan Bakery. (She could tell that he knew very well who she was and where she worked.) "Tell me how much bread you guys need and we can bake it right now. We can do it supercheap. Just at cost for materials."

April turned around to look at Joseph, who caught her eye with his dark, confident green-eyed gaze for a moment.

"I can bake it myself. Just tell me what you need and when you need it."

The old man looked directly at April and, in a voice that was higher and gentler than she was expecting, murmured quietly, "That's very kind of you."

He drifted back into the kitchen and huddled with one of the older women. He scribbled something on a sheet of paper, returned to the register, and handed the slip of paper to April.

"Thank you," he murmured.

April rushed out of the diner, intentionally brushing by Joseph on her way out, and jogged back to the bakery.

"Are you *kidding* me?" Carmen said, when April told her what she'd arranged. "You agreed to do *what?* And without asking me? Really, April?"

"Really!" April shouted back from inside the kitchen as she grabbed a rolling pin.

* * *

The bread incident—or, as Carmen called it, The Miracle of the Loaves—brought April and Joseph closer again. April, inspired, had managed to bake more than two dozen loaves of bread for the Amish diner's event. At one point, Joseph had drifted into the bakery to check on her progress and found her running around the kitchen, covered in flour. He offered to help, and together they rolled the dough and sprinkled it with seeds and herbs. And everything they did, they did openly, because, for one brief moment, the Amish diner and Carmen's bakery, and Joseph and April, were officially in business together. Everyone knew that Joseph and April were sharing this kitchen, and they all *approved*.

At one point, as Joseph, wearing a Metropolitan Bakery apron, was pulling a fresh tray of hot and crusty and perfectly browned loaves of rye out of the oven, April, despite everything, couldn't help thinking to herself, *Maybe this is how it could be? Why not?*

That night, April was a hero to Joseph's relatives. With her help, they came through for their catering client: everyone at the event complimented the bread and asked for the Amish diner's business card.

Carmen was even more impressed, and grateful, when April brokered a major deal: the Amish diner would now buy its bread—for its catering events—exclusively from Metropolitan. This gave Carmen a much-needed cash flow boost—and at each event, a new opportunity to advertise all over town—just when her rent was about to go up. April had helped secure Carmen's business for the coming year.

April was beginning to talk about taking classes in baking, so that she could be more helpful to Carmen. And when Carmen replied, "If you really want to help me, take a class in business management." April returned the next day with a stack of informational printouts about courses in business management. April's case manager was impressed by her sudden ambition and was reporting April's progress to the court.

In the weeks that followed The Miracle of the Loaves, April and Joseph enjoyed an easy and comfortable rapport. Sometimes, on their breaks in the park, they would just sit silently together, enjoying each other's company, as though this were the most natural thing in the world.

During one of these moments, sitting together on a park bench, Joseph pointed to the book poking out of her purse.

"What are you reading there?"

"Oh this? I actually just finished it this morning," said April. "It's just something stupid."

"Nothing you do is stupid."

April burst out laughing.

"Oh Joseph," April said. "If only you knew. Here . . ." she said, taking the book out and handing it to him.

With great deliberation and intense concentration, which made April laugh, Joseph read the back cover of the book.

"Don't read it too closely now," April said, but Joseph, still studying the cover, didn't seem to be listening.

"He . . . goes back in time?" he finally said.

It occurred to April that the phrase "goes back in time" wouldn't mean anything to someone who wasn't raised watching or reading sci-fi and who'd never heard of *Back to the Future,* much less watched it.

"Oh yeah," April said. "So, like, he gets into what they call a time machine, like a little car, but instead of moving through space he goes through time."

April looked at Joseph. He still seemed confused.

"It's like, imagine that you get on a bus, but instead of arriving in Lancaster two and a half hours from when you departed, you arrived two hundred *years* earlier than you'd left."

"Oh," Joseph said. "It's a strange story."

"I told you it was stupid!"

Joseph looked at her with his big eyes and said, "I don't think it's stupid."

"Maybe that's because *you're* stupid!" April said, playfully.

Joseph looked deeply hurt.

"Omi*god.* I'm just kidding you! You're so serious!" April said.

But Joseph still seemed hurt. April threw her arm

around his neck, and pulled herself to him, so that she could look him in the eyes. Without intending it, her lips grazed his cheek and the corner of his lips. A sudden jolt shot through her body—and Joseph's body, too: she could feel him tense up.

"Hey," she whispered, her forehead pressed up against his head, her lips grazing his ear as she spoke. "I *don't* think you're stupid, okay? Not even close. I think you're the best person I've ever met. Not even kidding. I *love* . . . that you're so serious. I I– . . . like, really like you. You know that."

They sat in silence for a few minutes, watching the sky turn orange with sunset.

"We should go back," Joseph said.

The words fell on April like a heavy weight. A sudden gloom settled over her. She was scared that she had offended him. That she had created a distance between them. Or worse, that she had exposed the distance that already existed between them. That she'd broken the spell that had allowed them to ignore that vast distance. And now she felt forlorn. She tasted what it would be like to lose Joseph— what it would be like, when, inevitably, she would, in fact, lose him—and it emptied her out.

They walked back to the market in total silence, which only confirmed April's fears. With each silent step, she felt the distance between them grow. She wanted to stop walking—but what would that accomplish? She wished she could go back to the moment when they had arrived at the park, still living in the bubble of closeness that she had burst.

When they arrived at the marketplace, and it was time to say good-bye, April didn't know what to say. She was afraid to say anything. Then Joseph reached toward her, and a spark of hope flickered within her. Joseph reached for her book, pulled it out of her purse, and said, "Can I borrow this? I'll return it."

April wanted to say, "Keep it forever!" But she liked the idea of him returning the book, of his placing it back into her hands, of how that exchange would feel on her skin. She liked the idea of making future plans, any plans, with him. She liked the idea of sharing something with him. A secret.

"*Of course* you can borrow it," April said.

Her eyes were drawn to the book. She liked the way it looked in his strong hand. She tapped on the book gently, and, with that, immediately felt the closeness return; the bubble that she and Joseph had shared was back, fully restored. Maybe even stronger than before. April turned around, and, with a big smile on her face, disappeared back into the bakery, where Carmen, overcome with customer requests, eyed her suspiciously.

By instinct, April immediately grabbed her phone to text Rose to gossip about Joseph. And then she caught herself. The sudden recollection of Rose threw her into a sudden tailspin. She'd pushed her feelings about Rose so far down these days that when they popped up, the effect was of an ambush.

Which threw her into an almost physical feeling of vertigo. These sudden flashes of Rose unsettled her to the point that she almost lost her balance. And even though these flashes happened inevitably, daily, they never startled her less for their frequency.

But now there was a new feeling: she was beginning to resent Rose. As the days went by and the emotional ambushes continued unabated, she found she was starting to blame Rose. For disappearing. And for putting her through this hell. She loved her sister more than any person on earth and she'd also been, at various points in their relationship, angrier with her than with any person on earth. It was a typical sister relationship, in that way: the love was always there but so was the capacity for deep rage. She didn't love this about herself. She felt guilty about it. But even these feelings of guilt could be redirected into resentment toward Rose. If she felt guilt, well, that was Rose's fault, too.

Before April returned to her work, she walked around the kitchen, ripping down the two "Missing" posters of Rose that she'd taped to the door, muttering, "*God, what a drama queen.*" She wouldn't touch the posters outside, in the market and around downtown, but inside the kitchen of the bakery she decided she no longer needed to stare at that face. Or rather, to have it staring at her. As she folded up the posters and dropped them into the recycling bin, she felt an enormous weight lifted from her shoulders.

* * *

The next few weeks were some of the happiest of April's life. She made more progress on her court-ordered program of meetings and community service. With Carmen's help, she'd enrolled in a course on business management at Community College of Philadelphia. Fall arrived in an explosion of colorful leaves that, to April, felt like a celebration of her growing feelings. On one of their walks, Joseph reached down and took her hand in his. April was shocked. But even before her mind could register what was happening, her entire body came alive.

"Are you *sure?*" she said, with a big smile.

Joseph just looked ahead and nodded.

"I mean, 'cause we don't *have* to."

"I want to," Joseph said, quietly.

April stopped short, pulled Joseph's arm down toward her, grasping him by the biceps, which was even stronger than she'd imagined. On his biceps, her hands suddenly felt small. She squeezed his arm and looked him directly in the eyes.

"What did you say?" she said, slyly. "I couldn't quite hear you—can you say it louder?"

A small grin came over Joseph's face.

"I said, 'I want to.'"

"Want to *what?*"

"I want to," he said, taking her hand and lifting it. "I want . . . *this.*"

April realized that her face was hurting from a giant smile that she couldn't seem to tamp down.

They reached a small park and approached a bench, surrounded by a small family of geese. When they sat down on the bench, Joseph released her hand. But April wasn't having it: she immediately grabbed his hand, placed it on her knee, and held it there. He grinned and wiggled his hand free.

"April," he said, shaking his head. "We shouldn't."

This little park would become their destination of choice. They would sit on the bench, their bodies pushed up close to each other, and chat. Sometimes they would sit there for what felt like an hour, but was probably more like twenty minutes, without saying a word. Just watching the world go by together. Watching the same sweet old woman who fed the geese and talked to them as though they were her own brood. Watched the joggers, the children eating hot pretzels. They watched as with each passing day, more and more branches of the giant maple tree turned red, until one day the whole tree seemed a giant bonfire of color, emanating its own light.

On that special day, they sat on their bench, under the maple tree. They felt freer with each other than they'd ever felt, as though the tree itself were able to provide shelter from every problem in the world.

"This tree is us," she whispered to Joseph.

"I know," he replied.

Chapter Five

Rose could feel herself adapting to the new situation. She was alive. And no longer in pain. Nothing else mattered. She was adjusting to her new schedule, her new life. They fed her decent food. Sometimes she got leftovers from their take-out meals. They occasionally let her poke her head out of the window. She would be blindfolded, but she could feel the warmth of the sun, the sounds of birds, the rustling of trees. In a strange way, those moments were special to her, made her appreciate the trivial things of life that you don't usually notice.

She was, in short, comfortable enough to feel gratitude, even in captivity. In fact, more so in captivity. And gradually, because there were enough moments of grace, she slipped into a kind of Stockholm syndrome: the feeling of sympathy—or even, affection—for the very people who held her captive. Her desire to break free from her chains, or even to think about the world in terms of freedom, had evaporated.

* * *

Fall turned into winter. Even though the routines that April had gotten herself into were all completely new to her—new enough that it seemed as though she were living a completely different life—they also seemed right, right enough that they might last forever. It was remarkable how quickly she began to take it as a given that she worked a steady job, was staying sober, and that she was feeling excited about a relationship that, though far from ideal, was at least not abusive, but rather life-affirming.

It occurred to April that she might be happy. Or at least as happy as she could be knowing that, even as the seasons changed, her sister was somewhere out there, cut off and . . . who knew what. With all the good things happening to her, she could forgive her sister for abandoning her, a feeling that she knew was not rational. And she could once again get serious about the search for Rose.

Looking for Rose meant snooping around, asking questions, putting up signs, trying to push local reporters into covering the case, managing #FindRose social media accounts, even having some art friends do a fundraiser. Between all of that, her work at the bakery, her course at the community college, and her court-ordered program of meetings and community service, April was exhausted at the end of each day. She felt constantly anxious about Rose's disappearance. But, for the first time in her life, she also felt that she was doing everything in her power to actually live up to the Serenity Prayer she recited at her NA meetings: *God, grant me the serenity to accept the things I*

*cannot change; courage to change the things I can;
and wisdom to know the difference.*

She might not have accepted the things she
couldn't change (yet). But for the first time in her
life, she was really and truly finding the courage to
change the things that were in her power to change.
It might not have brought her complete serenity, but
it was helping her sleep at night.

And yet, just when her new routines felt settled
and healthy, something would happen to remind her
how precarious her life still was.

Shortly after the first snowfall of the season, as
she made her way to the bus after an NA meeting,
April was approached by a guy dressed in baggy
jeans and a baggier winter jacket. He'd been at the
NA meeting with her. She noticed him at the meeting
either because he was new, or because he kept giving
her long, significant looks. Usually she'd dismiss
this behavior as creepy. But there was something
about this guy that didn't read that way to her. He
seemed vulnerable, naïve somehow, maybe kind. So
when he approached April as she walked to the bus
stop, she was a bit surprised but not alarmed to see
him. That was, she didn't feel nervous until he began
to speak.

"I'm Kevin," he said, extending his hand, politely.
"But people call me Cappy."

"Oh hey," April said, without stopping. The two
of them were now walking side by side. He seemed
to be building up the courage to say something. April

was mildly amused but mostly annoyed that she would have to rebuff his inevitable request to get a drink or, even more vaguely, to "hang out sometime." He seemed harmless, but the awful ones often did. And she wasn't in the mood to manage some strange guy's fragile ego. It'd been a long day.

"I met your sister a couple of years ago," he said abruptly.

April was silent. Her mind raced. It was not what she'd been expecting him to say.

"How do you know me?" she asked finally.

"I followed you to the meeting tonight."

"*Really?* That's the best you got?"

April began walking faster. This kind of unwanted attention was one unfortunate consequence of going public as a family member of a missing person. She'd discovered that some men had the audacity to treat her *Find Rose* events as an excuse to hit on the missing girl's sister.

"I work with Ricky Devereux," he said. "Well, I guess I work *for* him."

"Oh," April said. "Sorry to hear that."

"Ha, right? I get it. Well, look, I might know some things that you're gonna wanna know."

A thought crossed April's mind: to take out her phone and try to secretly record the conversation. But then she remembered that her phone was dead.

"Oh really?" she said.

"Yeah, for real."

"So, what is it?"

"Well, first things first. You talking to the cops?"

"Ah, I get it now. Ricky's getting nervous. Did he send you here?"

"No, actually."

"Really? And I should believe you because . . . ?"

"Stick around and you'll believe me. Ricky would probably kill me if he knew I was here, talking to you."

"Well, why are you here then?"

"I got my reasons. Look, just answer my question: You talking to the cops?"

"No," April said. "They're useless."

This was only a partial lie. In fact, April had very much been talking to the cops. But the conversation had run its course. The night after Ricky had dropped by the bakery and threatened her, she'd written a long, detailed description of everything that Ricky had told her about his last encounter with Rose: the date, the circumstances of it. She'd gone directly to the police with it, and laid out the whole story, along with her commentary, all the stuff she knew about Ricky and his motives. She told them that Ricky had texted Rose twice, and that he was refusing to show her the texts. Ricky, in short, was in possession of potential evidence. He certainly knew more than he was letting on, if he was not actually guilty himself.

April had given the cops the trail (Ricky) and the trail markers (the texts). She'd given them a lot. If they cared, they weren't showing it. When she spoke to one of the detectives, in his office, he didn't write down a single thing she said, even though she was giving them a lot of detailed information. As she spoke, she found herself staring at the pen on his desk, just lying there. At certain points she wasn't even sure he was listening. The detective seemed to be humoring her, waiting for her to finish so he could say, "Thanks for coming in" and then immediately forget everything she'd said to him.

April finally arrived at her bus stop. She zipped up her coat all the way and readjusted her scarf to keep out the wind. She wasn't in any mood to chat with this Cappy, if that was even his name. She began impatiently looking for the distant headlights of the bus, so that she could get away from this guy and get to bed.

April sighed and looked back at Cappy, hoping that he'd be gone. He was not. He just stood there, with his kind eyes, and his mouth, slightly ajar, like a patiently eager dog.

"Well," she said, "what is it? What is it that you got to say?"

"I don't know where your sister is at. But I know a guy who does."

April, who'd begun looking out for the bus headlights again, had heard but not quite processed what he'd just said. She was really too tired to puzzle out this stranger's motives.

"What do you want from me?" she said, wearily.

"Nothing," Cappy replied, offended. "Just don't tell Ricky nothing. Don't tell him you ever met me. You gotta promise me that."

"Fine," April said. She was getting tired of people telling her whom she shouldn't be talking to.

Cappy gave her a date—early the next week—and strange, precise instructions about how to buzz up at a certain apartment building downtown, near South 4th Street, not far from where she lived.

"I don't wanna go into some rando's apartment," April said.

"It's the only way, April," he said.

She didn't like that he said her name. This guy was a bit too smooth. But she took down the directions anyway.

"Why are you helping me?" she asked.

"Like I said, I got my reasons. Just do yourself a favor and don't ask. Trust me."

And then he turned around and was gone.

Two days and a snowstorm later, April and Joseph boarded a Greyhound bus. It was their first trip out of town together.

"Where are you taking me?" April said as they took their seats.

They sat next to each other. But April could tell that Joseph was nervous about it. The first time they'd met, sitting next to each other on the bus, they'd been strangers—now they were anything but. The closer they'd gotten, the more uptight he'd become about being seen together. As he glanced up and down the bus aisle, April got irritated.

"Your pals aren't here, Joey boy," she said, "and if any of them show up, I think we'll *notice* them right away. You guys kind of stand out, you know." She gave his hat a not-very-friendly flick of her fingers.

When the bus finally departed, and the young couple was in the clear, Joseph relaxed a bit.

"I have a surprise for you," he said.

"Oh really?"

He pulled his small suitcase from under his seat and placed it on his lap.

"Open it," he said.

"Open it?"

"Open it!"

She opened it. And inside, she found, very neatly folded, a man's button-down shirt and matching blue trousers, tailored in the "Plain" style: all buttons, no zippers, and suspenders stitched in. The uniform of every Amish man. April put her hand under the clothes and reached around the bag. Nothing.

"I don't get it," April said. "Where's the gift?"

"Patience," he said. "The gift is even better than something that can fit into a bag."

"I'm gonna *kill* you," April said, a bit too loudly, and then, realizing that she'd turned a few curious heads from the seats in front of them, leaned in close to him and whispered, "I'm gonna kill you."

Joseph just grinned and turned to look out the window at the falling snow.

* * *

When they arrived at the Lancaster, PA, station, April stood up and began to gather her bags. Joseph grasped her wrist and gently but firmly pulled her back into her seat.

"We're not getting off here," he said.

"But I thought you said we were going to Lancaster. . . ."

"I know I did," he said. "But we're not getting off here."

"Oh, okay." April collapsed back into the seat.

Most people had gotten off at Lancaster; the bus was nearly empty when it arrived, almost twenty minutes later, at a bus stop by the side of the highway. Joseph had told the driver to stop there and when they did, only Joseph and April descended the stairs. The driver gave them a very strange look.

And then they were alone. For the first time.

Well, not quite alone, because a car or two would zip by every few minutes. But otherwise they were alone. April looked around. There was nothing. No buildings. No billboards. Just the clear winter evening sky, some patches of trees, and big open cornfields, covered in snow all the way to the horizon—untouched except for a few deer tracks here and there.

"Where *are* we?" April said.

"Together," Joseph replied.

April gave him a quick, knowing look. She liked that he'd said that. No, actually, she *loved* it. But she wasn't about to let him know that.

Instead, she said, "Okay, this is just creepy."

They stood in silence for a few long moments.

"Okay, seriously, what's going on here?" she said, looking out toward the horizon. "Are you going to kill me or something? I knew it was creepy when you were like 'Let's go out into the . . .'"

April turned around. Joseph was gone.

"Hey! Where are you? This isn't funny, Joseph Young!"

"Right here," he said.

Joseph was standing about twenty feet into the little wooded area that separated the highway from the cornfield.

"Follow me," he said, motioning her toward the woods. And when she hesitated, he smiled and urged her some more.

"C'mon, it's fine."

"Okay, now you're seriously creeping me out," April said, as she walked slowly to him. "I'm from South Philly, dude. We don't do woods, okay? We like our trees where you can see them: one at a time, every couple of streets."

April joined Joseph under a canopy of thin, white-barked trees.

"Do you know what this is?" Joseph said, patting a tree trunk.

"It's a tree, Joseph."

"Do you know what kind of tree?"

"I dunno. A tall one? I'm cold."

"It's a birch tree. This one is called a gray birch. Its wood has a nice ripple figuring. It makes very beautiful furniture or indoor veneers. It's also good for firewood. But I don't like to use it for that. It's too special a tree to burn."

"Are you gonna kill me or what?" April said, as she began to walk again. "I mean, I know bowl haircuts are normal where you come from, but where I'm from a white boy with a bowl cut means you're a serial killer, okay? And this talk about 'special tree' is, for real, *creeping me ou . . .*"

April suddenly slipped on some ice and was about to tumble forward, when Joseph, in one long deft motion, quickly hopped at her and threw his arm around her waist, bracing her from behind. When both of them breathed again, they noticed that Joseph was, in fact, holding her entire body up, hoisting her about an inch off the ground. And for a long moment, he held her exactly like that, and she let herself be held. Except for their deep breaths, they didn't move at all. She felt his heart beating against her back, felt his entire chest moving against her back. Joseph was even stronger than he looked. He was holding her entire body in the air, and hardly straining at all.

And in this brief moment, her body went warm, then hot. Her hands were hot, her feet were hot. Her ears felt scalded. The sudden spike in temperature from very cold to very hot made April feel literally delirious, and suddenly the world turned and the white birches around her cascaded and the crunch of snow and twigs underfoot was suddenly drowned out by the sound of a loud beating heart that she didn't so much hear as feel thumping within her ears. Was the heartbeat hers or his? She closed her eyes quickly. She could feel every part of her body melting all at once. She felt she was powerfully powerless. And small but not diminished, an intensely concentrated sensation, like an atom that was being squeezed.

And then he let her go. Bringing her gently back to Earth.

"I'm sorry," he said, gravely. "I just . . . you were falling, and . . ."

Joseph turned away from April. She watched his large, strong back working out some kind of tension. He seemed to be speaking from some faraway place.

April didn't reply right away. She was still breathless from the near-fall, and even more breathless from the sudden feeling of being so close to Joseph's strong body. But Joseph interpreted her tongue-tied silence as disapproval or even anger.

And so he sputtered even more. "I—I didn't mean anything . . . I mean, I didn't . . ."

"Joseph," April said, finally regaining her ability to speak. "It's *fine*. I mean, it's really more than fine. You saved me. You're my hero!"

April took a step toward Joseph. They enjoyed another moment of closeness. And then he pulled away gently.

"Let's keep walking," he whispered.

"Really?" she said in a voice that was louder and

harsher than she'd intended. In the cold air and desolate woods, her voice carried and echoed, startling her.

She pushed Joseph away so hard and so suddenly that he almost fell back. She'd meant it to be playful, but a sudden surge of emotion had overcome her and her eyes filled with tears.

April didn't like how much power Joseph had over her, how physically overwhelmed she'd felt in his arms, and how quickly and profoundly rejected she'd felt when he'd said, "Let's keep walking." The swing of the pendulum, from feeling intensely warm and enveloped to desolate and discarded—and to not be even a bit in control of this shift—it was all just too much for her. If he felt even half of what she'd felt in his arms, how could he possibly just shrug and say, casually, "Let's keep walking"? Everything, to him, seemed easier than it was for her. Was he suffering at all? Was he feeling out of control? Was he feeling *anything?*

Fine, then, thought April. *Mr. Hunk Arms wants to keep walking? I'll take the lead.* April marched ahead, into the woods, without him.

"April!" he shouted after her. "*Hey.*"

She ignored him and kept walking.

"April," he called again. "You're going the wrong way."

She slowed down and finally stopped, sighed, and turned around.

"Where are we *going?*" April said, feeling her agitation deepen. "I'm cold."

"There," Joseph replied, pointing at a path that separated them. At the end of this path, she just noticed, was a horse, stamping its feet and snorting. April adjusted her eyes to make sure she wasn't seeing things. The vision of the black horse, surrounded by thin white trees and fresh snow, seemed like something out of a vivid dream.

Despite herself, April smiled.

"Okay, how'd you do that?" she asked.

"Had my cousin leave him here just before we arrived."

April gave Joseph a skeptical look and started walking up the path, toward the horse. Joseph suddenly appeared next to her and scooped up her hand. She pulled it away.

"I'm still mad at you," she said. "Even though you're a wizard and made a horse appear out of nowhere."

After a moment, April took Joseph's hand.

When they reached the clearing in the woods, she could see that it was more than just a horse.

"Omigod, is that a real buggy?"

"It's a sleigh."

"No, it's *not!*"

Joseph laughed. When he realized she was serious, he pointed to the runners.

"See, no wheels. This boy here glides on snow and ice."

"I guess I didn't realize sleighs were . . . a real thing?" April said. "I thought it was just like a fake Christmas thing."

"Only when they fly."

April walked around the sleigh and touched it, as though to confirm that it wasn't, in fact, made of gingerbread.

"So this is what 'a one-horse open sleigh' looks like," she said aloud, as though to herself.

"Exactly," said Joseph. "Except it's not open. I closed this one up. Warmer that way."

April was now on the other side of the sleigh. Joseph popped his head over it and gave her a knowing look.

April smirked but immediately turned and walked away. She wasn't going to give in to Joseph's charms so quickly anymore. She had to be more careful.

"So you're telling me you built this?"

"Yes. With help."

"What's the horse's name?"

"Elijah," he said. "Because he always thinks he knows what's best. And because of the chariots of fire."

"Um, explain."

"Elijah was a prophet in the Bible. He always insisted on being right about everything, even with God. Finally God grew tired of Elijah always insisting on being right and he took Elijah into Heaven on a chariot of fire."

"Got it."

Joseph was now standing behind April. She could feel his large presence looming and suddenly the heat was back. He wrapped his arms around her.

"Let's get in," he whispered into her ear.

* * *

The sleigh was so cute and cozy inside that April couldn't stop laughing. The bench was tiny, the doors were tiny, the door handles were tiny. It really looked like something built by elves.

"What's so funny?"

"You really don't see why this is funny?"

"No," he said.

This only made April laugh more.

But as soon as Joseph yelled *Yah!* and slapped the reins, sending the sleigh shooting forward, April immediately went silent. Her eyes got wide and her jaw dropped. She quickly turned to look out the window, and stared hard at the sleigh's runners, at the ground.

"Joe, are we still on the ground? Are we . . . are we . . . *flying?*"

Now Joseph laughed.

"Nope," he said. "Still on the ground. I hope."

He turned to April and gave her a long, tender look. With his right hand holding the reins, he used his left to brush her bangs to the side of her forehead.

They glided faster and faster through endless snowed-over cornfields. With his free hand, Joseph unrolled a quilt and spread it over April's legs. But she hardly needed it. In the sleigh's little cocoon of a cab, April felt perfectly warm and content. The night sky was clear, and the moon was setting, giving just enough light to create shimmering tails of glitter to the snow and ice. Faster and faster they went, frictionless, and it was impossible for April not to feel as though they were soaring at full speed into the deep. It felt thrillingly fast but perfectly safe. She suddenly found herself growing drowsy. The only sound was of the regular hoofbeats crunch-crunch-crunching on the fresh snow, a loud sound that somehow sounded small in the vastness of the wide sky. Within a minute, she was fast asleep.

When April woke—either ten minutes or ten hours or ten years later, she couldn't tell—she couldn't see anything: Joseph's hand was covering her eyes.

"Are you awake?" he whispered.

"I dunno," she murmured.

He removed his hand from her eyes. She gasped at what she saw through the sleigh's window: it was the universe. The moon had set and now they could see the whole of it, in its full, startling glory. They seemed to be floating in space, down the cascading Milky Way. The sky was teeming with life.

"Are we moving?"

"No," said Joseph. "We've stopped."

"I feel like we're moving, but *it's* moving, not us. It's even more beautiful than I imagined," she said, suddenly wide-awake. "It's so *alive,* almost breathing. I can't believe it. I can't believe it's real."

"It's real."

"I can't believe I've never seen the sky look like this. *Ever.*"

Joseph turned from looking at the universe to looking into April's eyes.

"Well, you're seeing it now," he said, bringing his face close to hers.

"I know. But . . ."

Joseph could feel the sorrow creeping over April's body and wrapped his arm around her and held her snugly against him. But he felt something in her harden. She suddenly tensed up, wiggled out of his grasp, and said, "I can't do this."

April reached for the sleigh's door handle, and said, "I'm sorry, I just can't." Then she cracked open the door and jumped out of the parked sleigh.

The untouched snow was light and fluffy and surprisingly high. April began trudging back in the direction from which they'd come.

Joseph popped out after her. For a moment, he just leaned out of the sleigh, watching her. April didn't turn around. Finally, when he saw that she wasn't turning back, he jumped out, into the snow, and began to jog toward her.

"This isn't real," she said, when Joseph came up next to her.

When he didn't reply, April continued. "See?" she said. "It *isn't,* Joseph. Just admit it."

"I think it's real," he said.

But this only set April off more. She stopped suddenly and crossed her arms and frowned deeply.

"Don't mess with me, Joseph."

"I'm not," he said, "I really like you."

"Uhh," April said, throwing her head back. "You don't even know me. You really don't."

"Well, I'm trying."

"Stop saying the right thing."

Joseph didn't know how to reply to that.

"Look," April said, "you don't know things about me. Ugly things, okay? Stuff you probably can't understand. I've been into bad things. I've had bad boyfriends. Like, *really* bad. These are bad people."

"I'm not as simple as you think I am," he replied.

"Let me finish."

Joseph nodded. "I'm sorry."

"I have to go to court every two weeks. I have a case manager, provided by the state. I could land in *prison* if I make one more mistake. Do you understand?"

Joseph looked at her but said nothing. She went on.

"I have to attend NA meetings, okay? That stands for Narcotics Anonymous. Drugs, Joseph. Got it? I first started using when I was twelve years old. I have a problem. I'm sick, Joseph. I'm disgusting, I'm ugly . . ."

April was crying now.

"No, you're not," Joseph said. "You're beautiful."

"I'm just trying to survive, okay? I live in a gross apartment, surrounded by gross, sick people, and I'm just trying to survive. I'm like a sick animal."

"April, stop it. No, you're not."

"I lied to you, Joseph. I'm not this cute, carefree girl, okay? I'm a liar. I'm sorry. But I'm not the person you think I am."

She broke down now and Joseph held her close. He said not a word but offered up his strong body to give her strength to stand. He let her cry for a moment and then whispered in her ear, "April, you are a precious soul. You are my friend. I accept you exactly how you are. And I admire you for being brave and going to those meetings."

April cried more deeply now. And, after a moment, she looked up, as though weeping under the open sky had given her cries more room to escape and had let her sorrow sail somewhere far away.

Joseph loosened his hold on April. They were face-to-face. He wiped away her tears with his hands.

They stood, face-to-face, hand in hand, for a long minute. Their breaths were completely in sync. Neither broke the silence, because there was no need to say anything more. Without another word, they walked back to the sleigh, hand in hand.

A new easygoingness had grown around them. They smiled and giggled at each other, instead of saying words.

"I feel weird," April said, "like light and giddy almost."

Joseph decided that this was the right moment to show her one of his surprises. He reached up to the ceiling of the enclosed sleigh and, in one quick motion, unlatched and slid open the wooden panel, revealing a glass window.

"First Amish sunroof," he said, brightly. "Designed it myself."

"I love it!" April said, shifting to her knees and pressing her face right up to the universe.

"I made it for you," Joseph said.

Joseph reached into his bag and pulled out a book. It was the sci-fi novel that April had lent him.

"And before I forget . . . I want to return this," Joseph said, handing it back to her. "I loved it. Thank you."

"Joey, please," April said, pushing it back at him. "Keep it. It's yours."

"This book is what gave me the idea for . . . this. For making this sleigh. Making it for you."

April gave him a quizzical look.

"What do you mean?" she said.

"The time machine . . ." he began.

But April needed no further explanation. She understood everything.

The sleigh, the magical ride into the universe. The sleigh was their time machine. And it was the most beautiful gift anyone had ever given her. The most beautiful gift that anyone could give her.

April lit the tiny candle lantern that Joseph had built into the passenger side of the sleigh's cab. Then she lifted the quilt over Joseph's head, enclosing them, together, in a tent.

"Thank you," she whispered.

"Thank you," he whispered back.

They found each other's hands and squeezed tight. Without a word of warning, Joseph leaned his weight against her body, and with his other hand, cupped the nape of her neck, drawing her head toward his for a deep, strong, and intensely surprising kiss.

Joseph's strong arm held her firm, as firm as the bench at April's back. Everything about him was strong. His neck, which April had now wrapped her arm around. His jaw. His lips. Even his tongue felt sturdy, decisive. And hungry for her.

He pulled away for a second and gazed into her eyes. She wanted to return the look, to sink deep into him but she couldn't—her eyes wouldn't focus. They both realized, at the same exact moment, that they were breathless and panting. And, at the next moment, they both laughed together with that realization.

April's eyes shut. She was unable to speak. Instead she whispered, "More."

She pulled herself toward his head, and blindly brushed her lips over his, gently letting her tongue slide over his lips. And there it was again: the spike of heat.

After a few minutes, April, feeling intoxicated, suddenly realized how tired she felt. She inserted her head at the top groove of his chest, where his collarbone met his neck, and she smiled, thinking how perfectly her head fit right into this warm and very dear little nook in his body. In a haze of drowsiness, she felt Joseph readjust her next to him, and tuck the quilt around her. And as she heard the sound of the horse galloping again through the snow, she fell asleep.

They arrived at the house well after midnight. "Where are we?" April said, groggily, as the hoofbeats came to a stop.

April was confused, not just about where they

were, but when. How long had she been asleep? What year was it? She felt as though she'd been asleep against Joseph's shoulder her entire life, and everything else in her life, all the comings and goings, all the problems, had all been a dream. She imagined, for a moment, that Rose was fine and waiting inside for her. She felt, possibly for the first time ever, that she was really waking up, that this moment was the True Present Moment, more vivid than anything else in what she'd thought was her true life.

And yet, when she sleepily peeked out the window of the sleigh, and dimly saw an unlit little house—a house surrounded by empty white fields and nothing else—it seemed like a dream image, full of meaning and importance, but lacking in clear detail.

"Joey," she said, rubbing her eyes, "what is this place?"

"This is where we're sleeping tonight," Joseph said matter-of-factly, as he stepped out of the sleigh and began unpacking their belongings.

"Yeah, I got that," April said, stretching. With the sleigh door open, the winter air was streaming in, bringing April into consciousness. She realized that she felt incredibly awake and clear.

"But like, whose house is this?"

It was, Joseph explained, his sister's house. Or, rather, it was going to be her house. Joseph and his brothers had just finished building it. In a month or two, Joseph's sister, and her new husband, were going to move in. Eventually, they would build this homestead into a small dairy. In the meantime, it sat empty. Joseph, as part of his family duties, was supposed to make a caretaking trip here every week or two, to check on it and make any necessary repairs. For tonight, it would serve as Joseph and April's refuge.

Joseph had a fire going even before April had unzipped her bag. The home was almost impossibly cozy. Everything—cabinets, tables and chairs, walls, floor, ceiling, and rafters—was simple, sharply cut, lightly polished heavy hardwood. There were iron utensils, pots, and pans hanging on the wall. The downstairs was a single-room space anchored by a wide fireplace that you could almost fit into without having to crouch. A potbellied oven crouched in a corner. The house smelled of fresh pine and fir.

"So you really built all this?" April said.

"Yup, me and my brothers," he said. "Still need to paint the walls. I wanted to do linoleum floors, but my sister wanted it all wood. So here it is."

"I'm with your sister," April said. "It looks like a house from a fairy tale."

Joseph stopped fussing with the fire and looked around curiously. Then he looked at April and smiled.

"I like trying to see things the way you see them," he said.

April curled up on a thick rug, next to the fire and watched as Joseph walked around the space, setting up house.

"You look really Amish right now," she announced,

as he picked up a heavy pail, poured water from it into a kettle, then set the kettle on a hook over the fire. "And really manly."

Joseph suddenly seemed to remember something. He reached into his bag and pulled out a bottle of milk and a couple of chocolate bars.

"Want some hot cocoa?" he said.

But April was up on her feet, feeling energetic, and not ready to get cozy. She was holding her phone, on which she'd found the song that had brought them together—that first time, on the bus—that fun country song, "Louisiana Woman, Mississippi Man." She played it at full volume and put her phone down on the table.

"Dance with me, country boy!" she shouted as she grabbed Joseph and began her best country two-step. Joseph was lighter on his feet than April had expected, and the two of them danced and laughed until they were out of breath.

After some hot cocoa, it was time for bed. Joseph produced a cotton nightgown for April. In his big strong hands, the nightgown looked so tiny and delicate, like a gentle sleeping ghost.

Joseph slept on the floor that night. Even though she was exhausted, April couldn't sleep at first. She was too agitated thinking about Joseph, about how he looked when he gazed at her, how he'd looked, glimmering in the snow, when she was pouring her soul out earlier that night, under the winter sky. It was true that he still didn't know the whole story—didn't know all the gritty details of April's life—but even so, Joseph hadn't flinched when she told him about prison, about the drug problem. No, he didn't flinch at all. In fact, what he had said—right there, on the spot—was more beautiful than anything anyone had ever said to her.

As she lay in the dark, thinking about Joseph's words, hearing them again in her ears—hearing how they sounded floating in the thin winter air—tears came into her eyes again. She rolled over and looked at Joseph, lying on the floor, his head propped up against a rolled-up rug, asleep. What was he dreaming about? April gazed at him and thought so many softly loving thoughts about her Joseph.

April, he had said, *you are a precious soul. You are my friend. I accept you exactly how you are.*

Those weren't just words. They were a bond that she recognized because she felt it deeply in her heart. As she lay in bed, drowsy, April gazed at the bedstand and saw the time-travel novel that she'd given Joseph as a gift, the book that had inspired him to bring her to this remote house on a sleigh he'd built with her in mind. That sleigh really was a kind of time machine that had transported them into some realm completely separate from the world, which belonged to them alone.

April felt loved, in this little home, in this little bed. That was all there was and all there needed to be.

Good night, sweetness, she whispered in the air.

Joseph murmured from his spot on the floor.

With only the occasional crackle of the fire and the rustling of the wind cutting through the deep silence, April felt totally safe next to Joseph—many miles, and somehow also many years, away from any worries. And in feeling so deeply safe, she finally realized just how lost she'd been. Lost for how long? Her whole life, probably. And yet there was so much more life left, in front of her. Tears filled her eyes and she fell asleep. April cried gently all night, cried even in her dreams, gentle tears of joy. Joy also because she began to believe that she would be reunited with Rose. This happiness was not like before, when she was in denial about her sister's absence. Now she found the courage to believe that Rose could be found and returned by the power of love.

And the next morning, April emerged from this river of tears, newly born.

The next week, April made her way to the address that the strange guy at the bus stop had told her about—Cappy was his name, she now remembered, as she approached the building on South 4th Street. He'd told her that someone in this building knew where Rose might be. April found that hard to believe. It was more likely that this Cappy character was full of it. Or worse: this was some kind of trap. Or some effort by Ricky to spy on her or intimidate her.

She'd thought of bringing Joseph on this mission but decided against it. She didn't want him involved in this. And didn't want to anger whomever this person was.

April followed the strange directions that Cappy had given her. She buzzed apartment 4D three times in rapid succession. Then she stepped away from the building—to where she could be seen from above— looked up the side of the building and waved twice. She did this and got no response. She waited for a minute. Then two, then five. She went through the process again. Twice. Nothing. After almost half an hour of waiting, she left.

Rose could tell that something had changed with her captors. They were now nervous all the time. Less talkative with her. More suspicious. And suddenly, angry. At first, they seemed generally angry. Then it became clear that they were angry *at her*.

Earlier, they had been mostly cordial, business-like. Some were even friendly. There was some sense that she was just a pawn in some larger game. But that had all changed. Now they were blaming her. It was as if they'd discovered something new, something that completely altered their view of her.

"We know everything," one of them had said to her one morning as he dropped a dog bowl of water for her to drink from. "*Everything.*"

She had no idea what they could be talking about. But whatever it was, it was bad.

Earlier, they'd shackle and blindfold her only when she was being transported somewhere, but in her cell she'd be free. Now, they'd often leave her for hours, shackled and blindfolded in her cell. For no reason but malice. They'd talk about her, in front of her, as if she didn't exist and couldn't hear them. They never used to skip feedings or bathroom breaks. Now, they'd routinely "forget" her for hours. Whatever routine had previously existed was now null and void: everything was unpredictable.

Once, one of the men came in to drop off her dog bowl of water, and then kicked it over as he walked out. She could hear the laughter from the other side of the door as she dragged herself over to the puddle of water on the floor and licked it clean.

Every moment brought new fears. She had no idea what was coming next. Or worse: she had a deepening certainty that she knew exactly what was coming. With each missed meal and each long stretch without any sign of life outside that heavy, locked door, Rose couldn't help but wonder if this was . . . *it*. Whether, this time, they were not coming back with food. Whether they'd moved on for good this time and left her here to die in this windowless room. She was honestly surprised every time they did show up again.

Hunger and thirst deepened. It was the thirst that was most brutal, leaving her to suck on the concrete wall for any moisture. Reality began to blur again, as it had when she'd first landed in the concrete room. When one of the men entered the cell, he wouldn't seem real to her. But then she would convince herself that he was, of course, real. But later, she wasn't sure. And she would recall things that were said but later wasn't sure whether it was all entirely in her imagination. She distinctly remembered one of the men saying to another, *We'll be done with her soon.*

Had he really said that? She closed her eyes to recall the whole scene. They'd come in to clean the cell. They were disgusted by her. And they let her know that by the grossed-out sounds they made. They blamed her for the conditions they'd put her in. One of the men became angry. And the other had said to him, *Don't worry, we'll be done with her soon.*

He'd definitely said that, Rose thought.

The thought didn't scare her, though. Not anymore. She'd begun to deeply desire death. On another day—was it the next day, or a week later?—she lay curled up on the ground as one of the men came in to drop off the water bowl.

Kill me, she whispered.

The man ignored her. She said it again. Again, he ignored her. She said it again. Finally, he said, "*Shut up.* Boss wants you alive for another couple days."

Chapter Six

Carmen could tell that something had changed between April and Joseph. In the days after Joseph and April had returned from their excursion to the cabin, a palpable electricity had overtaken their relationship. You could almost see the currents running between April and Joseph when they were within feet of each other. April hadn't told Carmen about the cabin, but she didn't need to. It was, to Carmen, completely obvious.

Though her friendship with Carmen was strong, April had long ago realized that confiding in Carmen about Joseph was not a good idea for anyone. It left them both feeling upset, and nothing good seemed to come of it. They both observed an unstated agreement not to bring the relationship up as a topic of conversation. Carmen was trying to honor April's decision, as an adult, to pursue this thing with Joseph, and April appreciated Carmen's effort. It was April's life, after all, and wasn't she entitled to make the mistakes of youth? Wasn't this how Carmen herself had learned about life?

Deep down, Carmen could admit that part of her unease with Joseph was simply that she felt jealous because he got to spend more time with April. Each time April ripped off her apron and threw it on the hook next to the counter and almost literally ran to Joseph, Carmen felt a small but distinct pang of rejection. Did April ever throw everything aside and run to see *her?* Did April even *like* her? Carmen was sensible enough to know that these feelings were unreasonable and yet, she was honest enough with herself to recognize them as very real feelings to her.

Joseph and April were finding more ways to spend private time together. Joseph was coming up with more excuses to "make repairs" to the cabin, and he'd bring April with him. And, by spinning a few stories to his relatives—making one group of cousins think that he was staying at the other's, and vice versa—Joseph was occasionally even able to stay, undetected, at April's apartment in South Philly for the night. He hated lying to his family, especially because they were so trusting. Despite his obvious closeness with the strange girl from the bakery, Joseph's family would never have suspected that he was staying at her house. The idea seemed crazy and inconceivable even to Joseph himself.

April's roommates—two scruffy guys who just happened to be named Bill and Ted—looked on in amazement at the tall, handsome Amish man who occasionally materialized in their hallway.

April liked watching Joseph interact with her roommates. Because they were often alone, she hadn't had much experience seeing him interact with people. She observed him closely. She saw how gentle he was with these two dumb boys who shared her apartment. He seemed amused by them, but without any judgment. He was kind. He listened, with real curiosity, to every inane thing that came out of their mouths and responded as though it weren't. He seemed much older than they were, even though he wasn't.

Joseph naturally gravitated toward the kitchen. Without being asked, he'd begun preparing food. He'd rooted through the slime of their refrigerator and the chaos of their cupboards, somehow digging up some food items that he could creatively mix into a meal. After quickly and meticulously washing some potatoes, and setting them to boil, he carefully removed the piles of junk that covered the table and set places for each person.

"We gonna eat . . . *dinner?*" Ted said. "Like, together?"

"Yup," Joseph said, smiling at the look on Bill's face, as he stood in the doorway, watching in mute confusion. "Family supper," Joseph said.

April caught Joseph peeking at her when he said the word *family* and she returned his gaze with a crooked and skeptical look. But her heart also jumped a bit. And she had to work to unbend a little smile that crept onto her face.

She noticed that Joseph, between his preparations and his listening to the boys' banter, was a bit preoccupied. She could tell that his mind was wandering elsewhere. At one point, she leaned in and whispered, "You okay?"

He replied, "Yup."

April had given him a look that Joseph, to his credit, immediately and correctly interpreted as "Don't you dare 'yup' me, mister," and then he said, "I just . . . want to tell you something."

"So go ahead and tell me," she said.

"Not here," he said, motioning his head over to Bill, who was tormenting Ted by throwing pieces of popcorn into Ted's mouth as he tried to tell a story about how drunk he'd gotten last weekend.

Joseph stopped chopping, wiped his hands on his pants, and turned to April. He looked at her, giving her his full green-eyed attention. That look that always caught her a bit by surprise, made her feel both self-conscious and also, confusingly, like dancing without any self-consciousness at all. Under that look, she always had to remind herself: *Breathe.*

"What! What is it?" April said, finally. "Why are you staring at me with that crazy hunk thing you do! Just tell me what's on your mind."

Joseph again nodded toward Bill and Ted.

"Later," he said.

She glared at him.

"I promise."

As April and Joseph lay down to sleep—April in her bed, Joseph on the floor, as usual—Joseph grew very quiet.

"So . . . what're you thinking about?" April said.

Joseph stared upward, directly at the ceiling, and said, "*I love you.*"

But he blurted it out in this odd, strained way—so it sounded slightly strangled and took on a tone that didn't sound like his normal voice. It sounded like some kind of movie alien had taken over his voice box.

April burst out laughing, and leaned over the bed to look at him. The wounded expression on his face only made her laugh more.

"Why are you laughing?" he said.

"Because," April replied. "Because I love you, too. Weirdo."

Ten minutes later, from somewhere deep under the blankets, April's muffled voice said, "Tell me a scary story."

Joseph paused for a long moment.

"I don't know any," he said, finally.

From under the blankets, an exasperated sigh.

"Uhhh. Don't be boring," April said, popping her

head out of the blankets. "Tell me a scary story or it's over between us!"

"Hmm, sounds tempting," Joseph replied.

April pushed a pillow into his face.

"Okay," he said. "I got one."

"Good," April said, and dove back under the covers, disappearing again. "That's more like it."

"This story is real: it happened."

"Really?" April said.

"Really. It happened. Years ago, but not that many. It happened in my family."

"For real?"

"For real."

"Whoa. Okay. What *happened?*"

Joseph told her a story he'd never before told—a story that, until this moment, he'd never thought of as *a story*. In his mind, it wasn't a story, but a hazy memory that lingered in the background of his mind like an old creepy portrait of a long-ago ancestor, a person without a name but with a strangely familiar face, that hung in your family's house, and whose presence was undeniable, even if it was never discussed.

"Hefsibah," Joseph said, into the air, after a moment. "That was her name."

"*Hefsibah,*" April repeated, slowly and gravely, as though reciting an incantation. She'd never heard of the name.

"Joseph, do I want to hear this?"

But Joseph was already telling the story, as much for himself as for April.

Hefsibah was the second youngest of twelve siblings, originally from Wayne County. The only younger child was a boy, who arrived maybe a year after she was born. One afternoon, when Hefsibah was twelve or thirteen, she collapsed during her chores. No warning. She just fell to the ground. She'd been hauling a pail to the barn, to replenish the goats' water supply. And the next second, she was lying flat on her face, with the overturned bucket beside her, spilling out its contents all over her dress.

Nothing would revive her. Not smelling salts, not cold water. As luck would have it, the family happened to know that a community doctor was nearby that day, making a house call at a neighbor's. So one of the young men in the house jumped on a horse and went to fetch the doctor immediately.

But the doctor, too, could not revive poor Hefsibah. It wasn't long until he determined that it was too late. She was dead. There was no pulse.

In those days, the Amish of this area rarely used the local hospitals. Usually they went to the hospital only for serious chronic illness or for surgeries. For most other cases, they used home remedies and their own doctors. In Hefsibah's case, they would have rushed her to the hospital, but sadly, there was no need: the girl was dead.

Hefsibah was buried in the family plot, behind the barn of the original family farm, which was down Stony Creek Road, only a short ride from where Hefsibah had lived with her family. Her extended family was almost too shocked to mourn. And, anyway,

Christian modesty and decorum were tenets of their community—every member of the family, following the lead of the parents, was committed to accepting this terrible loss as the will of God. Everyone but Gabriel.

Gabriel was the youngest of the Hornung family, the only sibling who was younger than Hefsibah herself. Only a shade over a year older than he, Hefsibah had been his best friend and closest ally in the world. Little Gabriel was inconsolable upon her death. He denounced, as a traitor, anyone who tried to console him. Worse, he cursed God. He would not accept the simple fact that his sister was gone forever. Someone was lying to him. And he wasn't having it.

After Hefsibah was buried, Gabriel remained by her grave all afternoon, refusing to leave. And when, one by one, his family left the graveside, his rage deepened. He couldn't believe that his family was just going to leave the girl outside, in the ground, like she was an animal. Gabriel vowed, then and there, that he would never forgive his family for this betrayal of his sister. They told him that she was dead. Her soul was in heaven. Her mortal life was ended. But, in his mind, his sister was alive. It was the rest of his family who were dead.

Gabriel kept his furious vigil into the night. It was a humid summer evening and he wasn't about to go inside. He curled up on her grave, on the freshly turned soil, and dozed off to sleep.

That's when it happened.

At first, he thought he was still asleep. But he wasn't. He was awake. He could see the sky and the dark shapes of the barn and pens and fields. He could smell the farm aromas. He was at his grand-folks' house. He was awake—no question about it. And the sounds he heard were real.

It was a low sound. The thrum of a heartbeat? Was it possible? No, ridiculous. Not a heartbeat, not a regular rhythm. But something. A distinct pounding of some sort. From the grave. Gabriel pressed his ear against the fresh, still moist soil, and put his hand over his other ear, canceling out all other sounds. And when he did, the sound he heard, from his sister's grave, was even louder and more distinct. A knock; then nothing, then more nothing. Another knock. Two more knocks.

"Wait a second," April said, putting her hand over Joseph's mouth. "What are you *saying,* Joseph?"

"Let me tell the story!" Joseph replied.

Gabriel lunged into action. He knew what he needed to do. He was a young boy then, only eleven or twelve. But he had a fierce personality and was also physically large. And the burial of his beloved sister—the unforgivable betrayal, in his mind, by his entire family—had filled his body with such a zeal-ous rage that, as people tell it, he became a fully grown man in one single night. When he heard the sounds—or what he thought were sounds—from his sister's grave, he ran to the barn, grabbed a pick and shovel, and began furiously digging. Though he didn't care for, nor trust, his family to help him, he knew that more people digging were better than one, and so he began shouting, even as he was digging.

It wasn't long before his uncles and cousins, and one of his brothers, came running out. Without even hesitating, they tackled him, certain in their suspicions that Gabe, already so troubled by the loss of his sister, had now finally gone mad. Gabe, who was strong, and so filled now with the righteousness and urgency of his cause, put up a formidable fight. But soon enough his family members overpowered and subdued him. They had to tie him up and gag him, though. He would not relent otherwise.

But when they had Gabriel gagged and tied up, and the noise and commotion of the fight had died down, they heard it, too. They heard the same sounds that Gabriel had heard, the same sounds that had sent him, deranged, into the barn to grab a shovel. The sounds were unmistakable.

"Joseph. *What* are you saying!" April protested.

"This happened, April," Joseph replied calmly. "The Hornung family is related to mine. We all know them."

The men and boys all stood there silently, by Hefsibah's grave. For one second they listened. And then it came again: the muffled sound of pounding. Without even saying a word to each other, they all ran to the tool shed, grabbed every pick and shovel they could, and furiously began digging. They were so focused on the sudden, horrifying task that they hardly noticed young Gabriel, still lying on the ground, gagged and hog-tied. But soon, one of them did notice and untied him. He immediately joined them.

Within minutes, they'd managed to dig far enough to hear more of what was happening down there. It wasn't just pounding. It was scratching. And most chilling of all: a small voice. It was a girl's voice, no doubt. But it sounded animal-like. No words could be discerned. And yet its meaning could not be more clear.

When they reached the casket—the very casket they'd buried only a few hours earlier that day—they hoisted it up and out of the ditch and threw open the top. What they saw in there was so horrible that none of them ever really managed to describe it directly. It was as if they'd forgotten what they'd seen, even though they hadn't, of course, but rather, remembered all too well.

All of the people involved agreed, though, that what they witnessed changed each person there that night, each in his own way. None of them was ever the same. And they also agreed on another detail: Hefsibah's eyes. Yes. They were wide-open. Wide, wide-open. And her lips murmured continuously. Every few moments her mouth would drop open, and her eyes would screw up, as though she were shrieking. But not a sound was heard.

The moment they'd come face-to-face—again— with Hefsibah, one of the older boys, Gabriel's cousin, Reuven, panicked. Convinced that this was the work of the devil, he lunged at the girl, determined to suffocate whatever demon had possessed her body. The other men restrained Reuven. But he continued to rave that they had made a great mistake in unburying Hefsibah, they had to kill the demon, or immediately re-bury this body—or burn it. The men, though they secretly wondered if perhaps he was right, restrained Reuven and overruled him.

One of the men picked up the girl. Her body was almost totally limp, despite the intense alertness of her eyes. He carried her into the house. It is said that when Hefsibah's grandmother saw this, saw one of the boys walk into the kitchen with the girl they had buried that morning, she collapsed on the floor and fell ill for a week. She nearly died, they say.

Hefsibah lived out the rest of her life on Stony Creek Road, just a short distance from where she'd been buried. She was eventually married, had a few children of her own, and lived a life of average length. But she was a strange, quiet woman. She said almost nothing. She never smiled. She had a look of doom permanently on her face.

"I saw it myself," Joseph said. "She would look at you and just keep on looking and looking, with huge eyes, like a barn owl, like she was looking into your soul. We were terrified of her. People said she could read your mind. But these were just whisperings. Because, of course, we don't believe such things."

Hefsibah died—for real—just last year. Joseph had been at her funeral. Her second funeral.

Lying in the dark now, April was so quiet that

Joseph thought she'd fallen asleep. But April was awake, though in a very strange state, almost in a trance. In the dark it seemed she was looking at the flat surfaces of Hefsibah's impenetrable eyes, and she could not look elsewhere. Joseph suddenly regretted telling her about Hefsibah, even though she'd asked for a scary story.

"Are you okay?" he whispered.

"Oh, Joseph," April replied after a moment. "My sister. Where *is* she?"

"I shouldn't have told you that story," he said. "I'm really sorry."

"No, no," April said, suddenly sounding more like herself.

She reached for Joseph's hand and squeezed it tightly.

"I'm happy you told me that story. Seriously. It feels like . . . I don't know. Like it's important somehow. It really happened. To your family. And that makes it important."

April and Joseph lay together in the dark. And then they drifted into sleep together, still holding hands.

In the bright morning light of the next morning, everything seemed very tender and still. Like all scary stories told at night, the fear and anxiety, conjured so fully in the darkness, also drained away fully with that darkness, and the new day felt brighter and safer than ever. Lying on the floor beside her bed, only just awakened, Joseph's large body looked so manly, and his morning face so sleepy and boyish. April could not have been happier.

Could this be the serenity that she'd sought so long in the Serenity Prayer? As she went into the kitchen to put together some breakfast, she thought about that word—*serenity*—and decided it was a lovely word. And that if she and Joseph ever had a child together, the child would definitely be a girl, and they would name her Serenity. *Serenity Young*.

She opened the freezer and grabbed the small container where she kept her coffee grounds. The smell of coffee reached her, and she felt even better, knowing that, in addition to having all these happy morning thoughts, she was also about to get some much-needed caffeine.

In her excitement, she almost missed the quirky thing sitting in her freezer. One of her silly roommates, no doubt, during one of their dumber moments, had accidentally put his sweater in the freezer. And like a total freak, he'd meticulously folded it up. April grabbed the sweater and pulled it out. It was stiff, as though it had been in there for a few days. April giggled to herself.

But then she stopped dead.

She quickly brushed off the sweater. She recognized it. The sweater didn't belong to her roommates. No. It belonged to Rose. It was, in fact, her favorite sweater: blue and gray with a pattern of small elephants. There were a few little snags in it, under the collar, left by Rose's cat, Dexter. A cold sweat gripped

April. She felt as though she might collapse. She shook the sweater, to remove ice. A note fell on the floor. It had two words written on it: *STOP LOOKING*.

April didn't see much of Joseph for the next week or so. She didn't have any clear reasons to avoid him—no good excuses for him, when he would swing by the bakery to check on her. She simply didn't feel up to it. It made no logical sense, but, in a way, she blamed him for the horrifying experience of finding Rose's favorite sweater neatly folded in her freezer. When she'd cried out and fallen to the ground—at first too terrified to make another sound, and then finally overwhelmed by grief—Joseph was the first person she saw, standing in the doorway, looking confused. It made no sense, but seeing him there, and the fact that she'd been spending so much time with him—and enjoying that time— made her angry with him. And her reaction was to push him away.

Joseph, uncertain if these signals meant that he should draw nearer or give her the desired space, eventually decided on the latter: to let April be.

"I want to see you," he'd said. "I want you to know that. I *always* want to see you. But I won't bother you now. When you want to see me again—if you do— you know where I am," he'd added, pointing toward the Amish diner.

That had been almost half a week earlier. In the

meantime, April walked around as though in a daze. She barely ate or spoke to anyone. She went through the motions. Work. The college class. The NA meetings. But she felt completely unconnected to anything around her.

Another week went by. April had visibly lost weight. She shuffled around, her eyes glazed over. Carmen was worried but couldn't get through to April about even small things, much less the big pressing questions. From afar, Joseph watched, too, and worried.

One Monday morning, he showed up in the bakery. Carmen, usually a bit cold and formal with Joseph, was thrilled to see him. He was really the only hope of getting through to April. They took a walk. Joseph remarked on how unseasonably beautiful it was outside. April looked around slowly, bewildered. It wasn't that she hadn't noticed the nice weather, it was that she hadn't even noticed that they were standing outside in the world, that there still was a world.

They sat on a bench, warming themselves in the sun, under the wintry skeleton of their special maple tree.

"Sorry," April mumbled, tonelessly.

"You have nothing to apologize for."

They sat quietly like that for a while.

Finally, Joseph spoke up again.

"April," he said, "I want to help you."

"I don't need your help," she said, and crossed her

arms over her chest. "I was doing perfectly fine without you."

Joseph gave her a look.

"I mean, with your sister," he said. "I want to help you find her."

"Joseph, don't," April said.

"I can help."

"I really don't think you can. And, anyway, I don't want you involved with that."

"I'm already involved, April."

Joseph suddenly took April by the arm and gently pulled her toward him, looking her deep in the eyes. April struggled hard with her mixed emotions. She squirmed away from him.

"Look, I know more than you think I know," he said. "And I also know something—someone—who might be . . . helpful."

Now it was April who gave him a look.

Joseph had been doing some of his own snooping around, it turned out. And he'd discovered that he knew some guys, some Amish guys, who'd worked with Ricky, done some construction for him. These guys knew some things; they had seen some things. They were shady characters, Joseph admitted. Not the kind of guys he usually talked to.

But despite all that, these guys might be helpful. Joseph could set up a meeting with them. He and April could go out to Lancaster and meet with them.

April listened to all of this listlessly. Joseph's efforts moved her—and, yet, she was too depressed about her sister and too irrationally angry at Joseph to listen. But she owed it to her sister to follow all leads. So she grunted and shrugged and said, "Fine, I'll meet these people."

"We're *going* to find her," Joseph said. "We can do this."

For the first time in weeks, April smiled a bit. It was a tiny smile and then it was gone. For a moment their eyes locked, and they couldn't seem to unlock. April felt the warmth. She felt her body drawn toward him. Her hand drifted toward Joseph's, brushed it just a bit, and landed next to it. He withdrew his hand and whispered, "We shouldn't, April." April immediately rolled her eyes and jumped up.

"We will find her," he shouted as she walked away. She gave no indication that she'd heard him.

Chapter Seven

April surveyed the scene of her twelfth birthday party—which was far from being a celebration. Little April kept a close watch on her younger sister, Rose, who was starting to get fidgety and restless, and a close watch, too, on her mother, who was growing fidgety and angry. April often felt as if she had two younger sisters—or, really two daughters: one, the free-spirited, slightly hyperactive ten-year-old Rosie, and the other, a loving but sullen and unpredictable, occasionally just mean, adult-child whom she called "Ma."

But for this one day, her birthday, April wanted to be the daughter, the kid. For one afternoon she wanted to be the birthday girl, to have her mom and dad and sister shower her with gifts and attention and cupcakes, not because she wanted to feel special but because she wanted to feel normal.

But her dad was late. He was always late—if he was around at all. For her birthday, he'd promised to make the hour-and-a-half trip from the shore, where he lived with his girlfriend, whom April had once met (and whose giant hair and long nails she'd marveled at). He was now an hour late. Then he was two hours late. There was no word from him. As time went by, Rose started to literally bounce off the walls. And April's mom had drifted toward the high cupboard where she kept the vodka. She'd grabbed the giant bottle, and then disappeared into the bathroom—the only other room in the studio apartment—which was where she did her drinking, supposedly out of sight of the children. But April knew and always noticed.

For a brief moment while they were sitting around the table—that was, sitting on the edge of the bed, since there wasn't enough room for chairs—she'd believed today might be the day. Today was the day they could feel like a normal family just spending time together. But as soon as April saw her mom disappear into the bathroom with her vodka bottle, muttering curses under her breath, she knew it wasn't going to happen.

Rose was, for some mysterious reason, standing at the front door, shaking the doorknob with all her might, as though she were trying to escape, playing some sort of imaginary game. Her mother was behind the bathroom door, probably sitting on the sink—as April had once seen her do—killing herself slowly with that bottle. Once April herself had tried this drink. While her mom was showering, she'd climbed up to the high cupboard, and secretly sampled it, and had decided that it tasted like death itself. April was clever enough to know that this drink was her mother's crutch in life, but she could not understand why; how could this vile drink, this poison, be the thing that she so craved? How could this be the thing she cared about more than her daughters? How could the feelings of sadness and despair, rage and violence be the things her mother so desired in life? It was a mystery to April. On that birthday, her father was where he always was: somewhere else. And April was left staring at an unopened package of cupcakes, so pretty and pink, wrapped up and untouched.

As April sat on the Greyhound bus, headed west on the highway, Joseph could tell that her mind was far away. She stared out the window, trying to remember that scene, her twelfth birthday. Some details were coming back into focus; others remained hazy. Did her father *ever* show up that day? She honestly couldn't remember. She focused hard, tried to put herself back in the moment and remember. But nothing.

What she did recall was that she'd started crying that day. She'd sat at the edge of the bed—the bed she shared with her little sister—stared at the sealed box of cupcakes and began tearing up. Quietly at first, then loudly.

And then, all of a sudden, she'd felt a small, soft

arm, and then another coil around her neck. She'd felt her sister's hot breath, smelling of candy, on her neck. And she'd heard her, in her raspy little voice, say, "Don't cry, Ri-Ri. It's gonna be okay."

Did her father show up that day? April couldn't recall. But she could remember, with total clarity, as though it had happened this morning, that her sister, Rose, had been there, and that she was the one who comforted her that day. Rose had been there for her, always.

As the bus ride dragged on, another memory suddenly came to April. Even though she couldn't recall whether her father had arrived for her twelfth birthday, she did remember that he eventually did give her a gift that year. It was a sad little doll, the kind you can get at a pharmacy, between the magazines and allergy medicines. It was likely that he'd done exactly that: on the way to see her, he'd probably realized that he'd forgotten to pick up something for her, and he'd stopped at a pharmacy to grab whatever he could find that resembled a gift.

That gift, of course, had been all wrong. April was too old for dolls like this one, much less for a piece of junk with a creepy expression on its face. It wasn't remotely what she had wanted. She'd wanted to go to the zoo with her family. But that trip was too costly and also required more coordination than her struggling parents could muster. And so this was it. He'd gotten her a doll that was wearing a nurse's uniform because he knew that April dreamed about being a doctor. He was, in other words, *trying*.

April never once played with the doll. But she did keep it in a special place. Especially after her father died, suddenly, shortly before her thirteenth birthday. That stupid pharmacy doll, in a nurse's uniform, was the last gift she'd gotten from her dad. She wasn't ever going to let it out of her possession. She'd packed it away somewhere. She hadn't seen it for years, had almost forgotten about that doll. But now, as she sat on the Greyhound bus next to Joseph, it was all coming back to her, accompanied by a feeling of immense hollowness, of a sudden emptying out.

In a swirl of emotions, April felt the sudden need to return home immediately and find her missing doll. But this odd feeling shifted to finding Rose. As she sat there on the bus, surrounded by strangers, sitting beside a man from whom she was feeling more and more estranged, April felt overwrought, and maybe even a bit embarrassed by these runaway emotions. Before she sank any further into her troubled memories, she turned to Joseph.

"Hey," she whispered, taken aback a bit by her directness, by the firmness in her voice. "I don't know about this."

"About what?" he said, sleepily.

"This," she said, gesturing around them. "This trip. Just not sure it's a good idea."

This wasn't the first time they'd discussed this. Just yesterday they'd had almost this exact same conversation. And what Joseph had told her then, he repeated today: the man who they were going to meet had some information for them. He knew some things that, as he'd told Joseph, they "were gonna want to know." He had some information regarding Rose.

"But doesn't this guy *work* for Ricky?" April said. "You know what I think of Ricky. You know I don't trust him. . . ."

"It was only on a couple of jobs. . . ." Joseph continued.

"Really, what kind of jobs? Because the jobs Ricky does . . ."

"He helped Ricky do some construction stuff. That's all."

"Yeah, that's all he's *telling* you. . . ."

"Look, he doesn't work for Ricky. And he's not his friend, either. He overheard some things, and he thinks we'll wanna hear them. Let's just hear him out."

April got quiet for a moment. None of this felt right to her.

"How do you even know this guy?"

Joseph hesitated before replying. April crinkled her nose.

"Been making some inquiries around the community," he said, finally.

It sounded suspicious to April. And she felt that his hesitation was more revealing than his answer.

But she was already on the bus, heading into

Amish country, and so she decided to ride this out. She turned away from Joseph and stared back out the window, at the fields going by. She heard Joseph say, in a near-whisper, "Just try to keep an open mind."

She didn't reply.

Instead she returned to her memories. She remembered the nicknames Rose used to call her: Ri-Ri, and Apple (which she pronounced *appo*). Apple had been one-year-old Rose's attempt to say "April." It had been Rose's very first word.

And now she was gone. *Dead.*

Wasn't she dead? Nobody would say the word. Nobody wanted to admit it. But wasn't it true? Rose was never coming back. All of this talk about finding Rose . . . it was all delusional, wasn't it? For a brief moment, April stepped outside of her own head and tried to see herself as she probably seemed to other people. Didn't she sound like those poor, tragic moms you see on the local news, those people who look like they haven't slept or eaten in months? They clutch some smiling photo of their missing daughter, wearing her cheerleading outfit, and tell the reporter that they are "still hopeful," and that they know their beloved Angie or Katie is coming home soon. But the look on the reporter's face says: "You poor thing, that smiling girl is *never* coming home." We all know how those stories end. *The search continues,* the news anchor says. *The relatives are holding on to hope.* And then, three months later, that same anchor will

announce, *Today that search has ended—in tragedy.*
The body was found in a creek.

April could see this clearly now. Wasn't she deluding
herself? Rose was not coming home. Her sister was
gone forever. It was time to start accepting reality.

And it was with this sudden, unexpectedly sober
perspective that April now turned to Joseph, and
gave him a long, hard look (she tried to avoid those
sparkly eyes of his—which were always such a
distraction). After months of anxiety about her
probation, April was finally free. She was almost
done with the mandatory NA meetings and community service. Of course she could still do these
things—and, after developing the habit, she saw the
benefits of continuing this work—but she was no
longer required by the court to attend. She would no
longer have the threat of prison hanging over her
head. She could miss a meeting or two, or stop altogether, and no one would care. With more time
opening up during her evenings, she could now
pursue her recent idea, to become a real, certified
chef; she could enroll in a class at the culinary
school—which Carmen would help finance—and
get started right away.

Joseph had been more than encouraging of her
new ambition. He'd done what he could to help her
prepare for this fresh chapter in her life. They'd
shopped around together for professional knife

sets—a requirement for culinary school—but April had been so stressed out over the unexpectedly high cost that she returned home without buying one. And this anxiety then triggered larger anxieties. ("I don't belong there," she'd said.) But Joseph had gone to work.

A week later, he showed up to find April, covered in flour, busy in Metropolitan Bakery's kitchen, anxiously practicing for culinary school. Every day, after hours, she'd been rehearsing various basic cooking techniques and recipes, in her furious and desperate and, in her mind, hopeless effort to catch up with what she imagined were classmates who were far ahead of her. Joseph walked into the kitchen that evening with a brand-new set of knives for her. He had made them himself, in a blacksmith shop, and engraved them with her initials.

"How'd you know how to make these?"

April pulled out a paring knife, admiring its craftsmanship. It felt both heavy and somehow also very mobile at the same time, just like the fancy Japanese knives she'd examined at the store a week earlier, the ones she could never hope to afford.

"My uncle used to do some bladesmithing," Joseph said. "Taught me when I was a kid."

"Of course you're secretly a master bladesmith. Should have guessed!"

And just as Joseph had begun to protest that he was by no means a master, April had thrown her arms around him and hugged him so hard that the tears that had welled in her eyes rolled down her face. He had seemed surprised, unprepared for her emotional response. In his mind, the gift was simply a practical solution to a problem: she needed knives and so he'd made her a set of knives. No big deal.

"Oh, Joseph," she said. "It's so . . . sad."

"What is sad?" Joseph asked.

But April didn't have the heart to reply.

Joseph had been such a positive force in her life at exactly the moment she'd needed it. If she'd gotten mixed up with her usual type of boyfriend, some pretty-faced lost boy, some addict, she wouldn't be sober now. There was no doubt about that. She'd have begun using again, which meant she'd be in jail by now. Joseph had been a steadying force. That was real. The results were clear. She'd made the right decision with him.

But that didn't mean it could last. It didn't mean the relationship had a future. She loved Joseph and would always love him for being a kind of guardian angel when she needed one, but the time had come to loosen their bonds, to begin the process of pulling away from each other. There was no future for them. No way forward.

And once April began to pull away from Joseph, she began to see him in a different light. She grew suspicious of him. Especially of his insistence that they meet this shady associate of Ricky's. What was that about? Joseph's belief that this meeting would help them find Rose seemed, to April, naïve. She feared the trip would be a foolish waste of time at best, and, at worst, reckless and dangerous. Who was this man? What was his agenda? April resented Joseph for dragging her out and putting her in danger, and that resentment was making it easier for her to pull away from Joseph for good.

April didn't want to be on this bus. She didn't want to meet this man whom even Joseph admitted was a shady character. She wanted to begin to deal with truths, even harsh ones. She was done with wishful thinking and delusions. And when she was entirely honest with herself, she could admit that the problem here was Joseph: he was just another delusion she'd had. And even worse—he seemed oddly sympathetic to Ricky, to the person who April knew was behind her sister's disappearance. As the bus hurtled down the highway, April made a resolution right there and then: yes, she would keep her promise and meet this guy. And when it was over, she'd turn over a new leaf in her life. No more sleuthing for a sister who was dead, and no more pursuing a relationship that was a dead end. When she returned from this trip, all of that was over; it was time for a new start, based on realistic expectations. She would push the cops to do their job looking for Rose. She would cut off all ties with Joseph. And she would begin culinary school and a new life. And she would continue doing the work to stay sober.

* * *

As they got closer to their destination, the stop after Lancaster station—April's silence deepened. Out of a sense of self-protection she'd decided to refrain from speaking, to harden her shell and just get through this. And her surroundings, the forest and cornfields, the big sky, only deepened her silence. The slow pace of rural central Pennsylvania gave her plenty of space to be alone.

They got off at the same stop they'd used on that magical night when Joseph took April on the sleigh ride through the snowy fields . . . but that had been a lifetime ago. April knew this was the same stop, but it didn't feel the same at all. Or look the same. They stepped off the bus without exchanging a single word. A horse and buggy was waiting for them nearby, left there earlier in the day by one of Joseph's cousins.

The buggy ride, too, encouraged silence. Without any explanation April slid into the cab, instead of sitting up front with Joseph on the driver's bench. He didn't protest, and it occurred to April that he was probably a bit relieved that she was in back, out of sight of the Amish community. April was annoyed that Joseph hadn't insisted she join him up front— even though she also would have been annoyed if he had insisted. The situation matched their relationship: there was simply no arrangement that made sense for them. It was a lose-lose proposition.

In the meantime, the pace of the buggy, the rhythm of the horse hooves clopping on pavement, gave her exactly the kind of peace she needed right then.

The ride was long but, as far as April was concerned, it could have gone on forever. But when the horse drew to a stop, April finally poked her head out from the window of the buggy, and she was struck by the feeling of being really deep in the woods.

Having been so entirely lost in thought, she hadn't quite noticed that the buggy had, many miles earlier, turned off the smooth, highway pavement onto bumpy unpaved country roads, and finally onto even more bumpy forest paths. April wanted to ask Joseph where in the world he had taken them, but she knew the answer: they were nowhere on the map. Suddenly, she felt scared.

Through the high treetops she could see that it was still a bright sunny day, but the foliage was so thick, that it was dark and dusky down below. In the deep forest silence, punctuated by the sound of a breeze in the leaves, April could hear occasional rustling sounds, the breaking of twigs, the sounds of little feet scurrying around. It creeped her out.

For the first time in hours, April spoke.

"Joseph," she said. "I don't like this. I don't like it here."

In breaking her long silence, her own voice sounded odd to her, strained, and not like her voice at all. Whose voice was it, though? The thought disturbed her even more.

Joseph leaned back and squeezed her hand—but that worried her, too. And she quickly pulled it back and retreated inside the cab. Even familiar things—especially familiar things—her voice, Joseph's strong hand, felt somehow wrong. Maybe she should jump out? Maybe she should run? Nothing here felt safe. Just as Joseph was about to speak, to calm her fear, they heard a voice.

"O'er *here*," it said.

April's mouth went dry. Her throat clutched shut. Joseph pulled the horse to a stop. She and Joseph turned around. Behind them, on the other side of the buggy, she saw a small hut—so small, and so much like a mound of earth rather than a human-built structure, that it was barely visible between the trees, even when she was looking right at it. And in the opening of this den stood a remarkably tall, alarmingly straight-backed man, his beard so long and wild that she couldn't quite see where it ended in the darkness. What she could see, and quite clearly, were two eyes, staring in a fixed and piercing glare, directly at her. This face wore no expression at all. The man seemed to want them to come in, but he made no gesture of welcoming them. In fact, he stood in the doorway as though to block the entrance.

* * *

Carmen was early to court. She was overeager. Today was the day that she'd been imagining and hoping would come for the better part of a year now: after a lot of hard work, many false starts and set-backs, April was finally about to gain her freedom from legal trouble. April was about to be freed from the threat of prison. Having completed her court-ordered programs, the NA meetings, the community service, after passing all her drug tests, staying out of trouble, and getting a steady job, she was now free from the court's scrutiny. She just needed to show up one last time.

And of course, she still had a record. Which meant that if she got in trouble with the law again, any judge would hold that against her. But April had served out her probation and she could now live and do as she pleased. Her time was, once again, her own. Unfortunately, on the day she was set to re-ceive her walking papers, she was nowhere to be found.

Carmen paced around the hall outside of the courtroom. April was only a few minutes late, but Carmen was already getting worried. Had April really come this far, only to mess things up at the very last moment? It seemed too crazy—or, unfor-tunately, all too possible, all too typical of April's history. What worried Carmen even more was that April hadn't replied to any of her texts that morning. Finally, Carmen walked up to the court clerk, who was growing tired of waiting, prepared to lie and say that April had just called her to say she was on her way, when April suddenly materialized at the end of the hall.

But was it really April?

Carmen squinted for a moment. It certainly *looked* like April, but she was walking really slowly, as though taking a stroll with all the time in the world.

"Get over here!" Carmen said, waving to her madly. "What's gotten into you?"

In court, Carmen couldn't stop looking over at April. She looked different. Not like herself. Emptier, somehow. Something had changed. Something had come over her. Carmen studied her face for clues. Her eyes were dull, her mouth expressionless. There was no energy in her shoulders or back. She seemed to be dragging her feet. Wasn't this a happy occasion? Wasn't this the day that she'd been looking forward to for so long?

During a pause in the proceedings, as the judge looked over some documents, Carmen leaned over and whispered to April, "What's going on with you?" April seemed pained to hear someone talking to her. Without turning to Carmen, April just shrugged. Carmen tried again.

"April. Honey. I know something's the matter. . . ."

"Tell you later," April muttered in reply.

Carmen caught the eye of the court clerk, whom she'd earlier witnessed impatiently kicking people out of the room if they chatted too much. She sat back and sighed. She'd have to wait for an answer.

Well, Carmen thought to herself, at least April had showed up.

As they walked out of the courthouse, April held her walking papers loosely, absentmindedly, as though ready to let them drop from her fingertips onto the ground and keep on walking without even noticing. Carmen quickly grabbed the documents, folded them up, and slipped them into her purse. She stepped in front of April, put both hands on April's shoulders and halted her forward motion. She held April in place and looked directly into her eyes. April turned to look at the ground.

"Before we get to what's eating you," Carmen said, "and we will get to that in a moment, I think it's really important to stop and acknowledge that you *did it*. Honey, you're free! You earned it. You did so well and I'm so, so, proud of you, kiddo. . . ."

April didn't look up or move. But Carmen could tell that she was becoming emotional. When Carmen took her into a big hug, the tears came freely.

"I know things are hard," Carmen said, "but this is a happy day, baby girl."

"I know," April whispered, barely audible.

After walking quietly for a few minutes, down a sun-drenched city block, Carmen took April's hand and said, "Do you wanna tell me what's going on in that head of yours?"

April must have realized that holding back would probably take more effort than simply coming clean. So she told Carmen what was going on in her head.

She told her about the trip she'd just taken with Joseph, to Amish country, deep into the woods, to meet the shady man whom Joseph believed could help them find Rose.

"*Why* are you spending time with Joseph?" Carmen said, somewhat exasperated. "You need to stop seeing him. That means totally. Even for Rose stuff."

"I know," April replied.

Something in the way April said it convinced Carmen that she meant it.

"Okay, good," Carmen replied. "I'm glad we're in agreement there."

April continued with the story. She told Carmen how the man looked: Amish, but in a weird, back-country sort of way, not like the well-groomed, polite Amish folks you usually see. He was more of a mountain man. He hadn't showered recently; his clothes were tattered and dirty; his beard was big and bushy. There was no sign of a family or a farm nearby.

Carmen nodded, knowingly. "Oh yes, I know that type. You don't see them in the farmer's markets, or around the general stores near Lancaster."

The meeting hadn't taken long, April said. This guy wasn't one for chatting. They sat down in his little hut, on ramshackle chairs around a ram-shackle table. There weren't even enough chairs for the three of them: Joseph stood the whole time. After sitting there, staring at each other in a long awkward silence, Joseph finally stepped in and asked the guy to say what he knew.

April, recounting the story, stopped. She just shook her head.

"What?" Carmen said. "What did he *say?*"

"Well," April said, slowly, "he said that, just a day or two before we'd met him, he'd heard Ricky talking about Rose. And from what Ricky said, it was clear that Ricky had no idea where Rose was."

"Hmmm," said Carmen.

"What?" replied April. "Do you believe him, this crazy beard man?"

"I mean . . ." said Carmen.

But April cut her off.

"Look," April said, "I don't trust this guy. Like, not at all. I mean, think about it, why was he even with Ricky to begin with? How does he even know Ricky?"

"That's a good question," said Carmen.

"Oh, I think it's exactly the question," April said, and stopped walking, which forced Carmen, too, to stop. "This weirdo in the hut? He *works* with Ricky, okay? He's basically one of Ricky's guys. I knew he was shady. But when I heard that, I was like, 'Oh, okay, it's official.'"

Carmen didn't reply, but just stood there for a moment, on a busy sidewalk in the middle of downtown Philly, as people walked quickly by them, while she thought about what April had just said.

"So you think . . ."

"Yeah, I think Ricky sent him. No question about it. I think Ricky sends these guys to me to tell me that he's innocent. To try to throw me off the trail. But it's not gonna work. How stupid does he think I am?"

Carmen, again, stayed silent, trying to process what April was telling her. There was one thing that didn't quite make sense to her, though.

"I get how upsetting this all is," Carmen began, slowly, choosing her words carefully, trying not to provoke April. "But I guess my question is this: Why are you so . . . thrown off by this? You seem suddenly out of sorts. And, I mean, this stuff with Ricky . . . it isn't new. You've been on to him for a while . . . so why do you seem so rattled about it this time?"

April suddenly became emotional again. Her eyes welled up. There was clearly more to the story, more that April hadn't said.

"What is it, honey?" Carmen said, putting an arm around her. "You can tell me."

"The creepy man," April said, slowly, choking back tears. "He wanted to prove to us that he was telling the truth. . . ."

She couldn't go on.

"It's okay," Carmen said, squeezing April's hand.

"He wanted to prove to us that he was for real," April continued, "so he went into his cupboard and came back with a bunch of things that belonged to Rose. Her shoes, the purple Keds that she painted herself. I recognized them immediately. And her feather earrings. He put them on the table. Just placed them there, without a word. And then looked at us. It was . . . so horrible, Carmen."

"Did he say where he got Rose's things? If he's just this innocent bystander . . ."

"Exactly. Oh, he simply refused to tell us. Said that he'd never seen Rose and had no idea where she was and had nothing to do with any of it. But that these items of hers had somehow landed in his possession. That's all he'd say."

Carmen and April arrived back at the bakery. They both put their aprons on and started working again, without saying a word.

"And the worst part is," April finally said, "I don't trust Joseph anymore. I really don't."

There it was, clear as day. Those words: *I don't trust Joseph.* They hung there in the air for a moment. Carmen was surprised to hear them.

"I've been struggling for a while now with this feeling," April admitted. "And now, talking to you, one of the few people in the world I really do trust, it's come clear to me."

"Oh," said Carmen, "I see. Well, that is a kind of big deal."

"I didn't want to meet that creepy guy. And Joseph kind of forced the meeting. And then, once we got there, and it was clear to me that this guy was just fronting for Ricky, I was really angry. And scared, too. But even then, Joseph tried to convince me that this guy was telling the truth."

"Do you think Joseph is . . . you don't think *he's,* like, working for Ricky?"

April just sighed.

"I know it seems crazy. But I just don't know. I can't be sure of anything anymore. Like, it's possible Joseph just got taken in by this guy. Which is a problem. But it's also possible that, yeah, he's actually working for Ricky. Which is way more than a problem. Ricky's sneaky. And, like I told you, he's been on some sort of a campaign to manage me. So I dunno. Maybe this is part of that."

"Wow," Carmen said.

"I mean, Joseph came into my life right after Rose disappeared, right? Maybe that's just a coincidence. And maybe it's also just a coincidence that Joseph, from the beginning, was very interested in helping with the search for Rose. And maybe it's also a coincidence that Joseph happens to know this guy who knows Ricky, and just *happens* to have inside information about Rose. But there's a lot of coincidences here. . . ."

April and Carmen silently kneaded and cut dough for a minute.

"And like," said April, "when this creepy dude carried my sister's shoes in his creepy dirty hands and dropped them on the table, I just turned to Joseph and looked at him. Just stared at him. And he looked back at me. But it was really weird and kind of scary. Because it was like I didn't know who he was, like he was a total stranger to me. I was sitting there shocked and kind of horrified to see my *sister's shoes* on this man's table and Joseph looked at me, totally unsurprised, almost casual. It was this distant, hard look. He seemed like one of them, Carmen. I felt this chill down my back, and I was thinking, 'Oh my God, you *knew* about this, didn't you? You were a *part* of this.'"

Chapter Eight

April walked a different way home that night. She'd begun doing this as much as possible: changing her walk, going a different route. Changing her routine. Stopping, on her way home, in the same corner store two days in a row, and then not stopping there for two days, then back to two days stopping there. The goal was to throw off the person who, she suspected, was following her around town—or else to help her to determine whether she was going crazy.

If she kept the same route for a few days, she'd see *him*: the tall, thin man with a baseball cap pulled low over his head. He'd be following her. If she stopped at the store, she'd lose him. Until she left the store, and there he was again. Until he seemed to notice that she was noticing him, and then he became more cautious—if she took an unexpected turn, or stopped at the grocery store, he'd disappear for the night.

Unless April was imagining all of this. It was

distinctly possible. But just when her inner voice of reason told her, *You're just nervous, no one is following you around, this isn't a movie,* she'd see him again, the tall thin man with the baseball cap pulled low.

Constantly in search of new routines to throw this man off, April walked into Bob & Barbara's, a dive bar on the corner of 13th and Walnut. She went in without hesitation. It was as if her feet were on automatic pilot. This place had once—and not that long ago—been her bar of choice, the place she'd stumbled out of drunk on countless late nights. She hadn't set foot in there in months. Usually, she avoided that block altogether; that's how recovery works, she'd been told. Just avoid the trouble spots altogether. But now, her feet carried her right in, stepping over the creaky floor plank and immediately sidestepping the bench near the door, which jutted out a bit too far from its booth. It had been a while, but she still had a powerful muscle memory from hundreds of hours spent in this place.

April sat at the bar, at her usual spot, and looked at the drink menu. It had expanded since she'd gotten sober. But everything else in the bar was unchanged. It was exactly as it had been when she'd last passed through the grimy door with the fogged-up window. So much had happened to April and yet, now that she was sitting here, it was as if no time had passed. It was as if she'd just walked out of the bar one night, for a short smoke break, and returned five minutes later. She inhaled deeply and took in a giant breath, filled with the familiar beer and wine and whiskey aromas. Her switch was flipped.

All of that mental momentum was leading her to place an order. It would be so easy. How was it *so* easy? The bartender, who was new and didn't recognize April, would just hand her a drink, like it was no big deal. Like it wasn't the end of the world. All she needed to do was give the word.

There was no question about it: she needed to get out of there. But she stayed. Her legs were not moving. Her brain was already tasting the sweet-tartness of a beer. She tried to fight it. She even stretched and reached for her coat. As much as she hungered for a drink, she'd also built up new habits, to redirect herself. And so she began to push herself toward her coat.

She tried her best. But just as she slipped on her coat and began to turn toward the door, April heard the voice of a young woman behind her.

"Hey there," she said. "Sorry for the wait. Busy night here. What can I get you?"

And just like that, April's knees buckled, and she collapsed back toward the barstool. All the muscle memory came rushing back. There was literally nothing in the world April wanted more than a beer. Just that first taste of it. *Maybe I'll order something and just take one sip and then leave,* she thought. *One sip!* She knew that was a lie. But knowing it was a lie didn't deter her. On the contrary, self-awareness somehow made the lie okay. And that's what scared her the most.

She sat on the barstool and spun around toward the bartender.

"What's on tap?" April asked.

April, unimpressed with the drafts, ordered her old drink. Muscle memory.

"I'll have a lager," she said.

In Philly, "a lager" always means a bottle of Yuengling beer.

The bottle of Yuengling came. April stared at it. It looked back at her, with its mouth open, awaiting hers. She passed her nose near it and inhaled its tart chill. And then April sat up, threw a ten-dollar bill down on the bar, told the bartender to help herself to the beer—that she hadn't touched it—and then she turned around and briskly walked out before the bartender could reply.

Outside, as she walked home, April sensed someone moving near her, in the dark. Was it *him?* She didn't look. She just steeled herself and started jogging toward home. When she got there, she quickly threw a glance over her shoulder. There was nobody there.

"There's something I need to tell you," Carmen said to April, then hesitated.

Carmen and April were cleaning up after a busy day at the bakery. April had been scurrying around, picking up trash, wiping down the tables and, in one practiced motion, flipping the shop's OPEN sign around to CLOSED. Carmen watched all of this with satisfaction and also some amazement at how natural it all seemed to April now, how much April had become a pro; she had come a long way since that first crazed day. Carmen was starting to have serious thoughts about her future with April. Maybe April could be a partner in this business . . . maybe, one day, she could take it over?

But that was a long time down the line. And, anyway, there were a lot of steps that they needed to take together before they got there, including some personal steps. One of those steps would happen tonight. Carmen now realized that the time had come for her to tell April the truth. The full truth. If April was really going to be a permanent part of Carmen's life, a part of her inner circle, she needed to know who Carmen really was. Or who she'd once been. Where she came from. It was time to tell her The Big Secret. Especially now, with all this Joseph stuff coming to a head.

"April?" Carmen said, hesitantly at first; then gaining more confidence, she repeated it. "April . . . stop for a second and come over here. This is important."

April put down the mop and walked over to Carmen.

"What is it?" she asked.

"There's something about me, my past, that I haven't told you. That you need to know."

Carmen paused. This was turning out to be harder than she'd imagined.

"Okay," she said, taking a deep breath. "I'll just say it: I grew up in Joseph's community."

April's mouth dropped.

"Well," Carmen added, "not exactly in *his,* but in one a lot like it. I grew up . . . Amish."

April just stared at Carmen.

"You know your jaw just literally dropped, right?" said Carmen.

"I just . . . wow," April finally said. "Not sure what to say. I had no idea. Why was it a secret?"

"I'm sorry I didn't tell you until now. I wasn't trying to keep it from you. I just . . . I don't talk about it to almost anybody. I don't even like to think about it myself, to be honest. There's kind of a story there, you know?"

And now, with the truth revealed, Carmen told her that story.

Carmen was born Abigail, the oldest daughter of eight siblings of the Lantz family, an Old Order Amish family, who lives near Bird-in-Hand, Pennsylvania.

Carmen/Abigail was the pride of the Lantz family and their community. The perfect daughter. And, of course, she was also a prized potential bride.

Abigail's charmed life got somehow even more charmed when she married the community's most-loved young bachelor, Jacob Thomas Weaver. Within a year of their marriage, Abigail had a beautiful healthy child, a girl, who arrived like a blessing to the entire community.

But a year later, everything went terribly wrong. A freak accident during a summer storm changed Abigail's life: in one afternoon she lost her beloved Jacob and her only daughter, Baby Rebekah, who was just learning to walk. Heartbroken and bereft, Abigail began a tailspin from which she barely recovered. Fairly or not, she blamed her community for the deaths of Jacob and Rebekah. And her family's heartfelt but, to her, inadequate response to her grief finally drove a wedge between her and them, and between her and the community. And between her and her faith. She felt the need to escape and start a new life.

So she did. Abigail moved to the city, to Philly, changed her name to Carmen—a name she'd seen on a bus billboard for the Philadelphia Opera—and she never looked back. Or, at least, she tried to never look back.

"I hope you can forgive me," Carmen said. "I hope you can see why I didn't tell you."

"Of course," said April, as she walked over to Carmen and put her arms around her. "That must have been so hard."

April tried to empathize with Carmen—but it was still a lot for her. There was so much she didn't know in her life right now: about Rose, about Joseph, and, now, also about Carmen. Throughout all the confusion, Carmen had been one of the few steady things in April's life over the past year, and now, it turned out that she didn't really know her, either. And not only that, but Carmen's secret crossed right over into the Amish world that had suddenly come to dominate April's thoughts.

Now April understood why Carmen had been carefully trying to steer April away from Joseph since the beginning. It wasn't because Carmen was ignorant of Amish ways but because she had her own baggage. Hearing the story of Carmen's own difficult path in life came at just the right moment for April. It helped her feel more confident about her own decision.

"But I'm still going to miss Joseph," April said when they talked about it.

"I know, honey," Carmen said, taking April's hand and squeezing it tightly. "But it's for the best. You're turning a corner now in your life and sometimes that's hard to do."

April, feeling like she was carrying a sack of bricks on her back, walked home slowly that night. She was trying to process everything. It was all so confusing. On the one hand, she felt as if her soul had been taken from her because of her sister's disappearance—and the slow process of acceptance that Rose might really be gone forever. And yet, April was healthier than she'd been in years—maybe ever in her life. She'd passed a major test: she'd been facing prison time, a completely different life path, but she'd stayed on course and navigated herself through danger.

Now she was sober—really sober. She had a job. She was about to take classes that would put her on track for a real career. Things might not have worked out with Joseph, it was true, and it was possible that Joseph was not quite who he said he was—but still, on a basic level, April had managed a healthy, non-abusive relationship. Her first. Even though the relationship had ended, it had been a kind of success.

April's new life helped her see that it was over, that it *had* to be over, with Joseph. It made her intensely sad, because she'd fallen in love with him. But it was the right decision and, for once in her life, she could take true comfort in knowing that a setback like this breakup would actually help her move forward and leave her stronger than before. Carmen was right. She was turning a corner in her life.

April was so busy with these thoughts, she'd hardly noticed that she was almost home, and was actually turning the corner onto her street. And that's when she saw him. *Again*. The tall thin man with the baseball cap pulled low. At first she heard his footsteps behind her. Then she glanced over her shoulder and saw him, walking twenty feet behind her. She suddenly had an idea. She stopped short and pulled out her phone. And when she did that, she heard him suddenly stop, too, and she knew, without any doubt, that this man was following her. Why else would he stop the moment she stopped? In that sudden hesitation of his footsteps, she knew she was being followed, and that knowledge terrified her and literally took her breath away. For a second, she felt as though the man were right behind her, grabbing her by the neck, preventing her from breathing. But there were no hands on her neck.

The man, probably sensing that he'd been found out, quickly resumed his movement. From behind her, April could hear his footsteps again. She turned around just in time to see him skip across to the other side of the avenue and disappear onto a side street. By the time April reached the front of her apartment building she'd managed to convince herself, once again, that it was in her head. That it was her anxiety and her generally heightened emotional state at the moment that had caused her to think this stranger's footsteps had stopped when she'd stopped. It was perfectly normal for a guy to cross the street like that. It was her own oversensitivity that made her hear it, and feel it, as something else.

So she convinced herself. But her shaking hand, working extra hard to fit her key into her lock, told her that she hadn't quite succeeded in convincing herself.

There were some practical things to take care of, regarding Rose—her apartment, for one. April had taken up a collection with Rose's friends to pay Rose's rent for the first couple of months of her absence. And when that became too much of a strain, she helped sublet her sister's room. She kept it as a sublet for a while—and kept all of Rose's stuff there—just in case she returned. It was really important to April to keep the place ready, so that when Rose came back, she had a proper home. Rose would need that stability more than ever.

But the months were passing by. Soon, it would be a year. Subletting was becoming a burden. And Rose's apartment mates, though they were too kind to say it directly, did not want to live among Rose's things anymore. They were getting tired of new subletters coming and going. The time had come to move Rose's stuff out, and to put the room back on the rental market.

April was also of the belief that this was a way of admitting that Rose wasn't coming back, though nobody would say it. Friends, who could read defeat on her face, would try to comfort April by saying, "This doesn't mean we're giving up. We're not giving up! When we get Rose back, we'll find her an even better place to stay." April, who was genuinely moved by these sentiments, would try to smile. But none of it changed the basic fact that Rose was gone, and that she would never again live in this, or any, apartment.

April had quite intentionally avoided Rose's apartment during her absence. She'd stopped by to pick up Rose's cat, Dexter, and bring him back to her place, and she came by to help show the place to subletters. But she never lingered in Rose's space. Every item, every stuffed animal, stabbed at her heart. All of the dresses hanging in the closet—each one so familiar that they *were* Rose—floating there like gauzy ghosts of her sister. She avoided them.

Friends offered to help. But April had always said no. This was her job. She had to return to that room, and to immerse herself in her sister's stuff, to undertake the painful process of packing away— burying—her sister's life in moving boxes.

Every item brought a world of emotion to her. Happy memories, attached to an old toy or an old concert ticket stub pinned to the wall, were the hardest to deal with. It was almost too painful to bear, that sense of bitterness and loss when she wrapped up the toy, or carefully removed the ticket from the wall, and placed it into a box.

And the pain was deepened by the loss of Joseph. She could really use his touch, his sensitivity, even just his strong, gentle presence, looming next to her. Someone to literally lean on. If they were still together, April was certain Joseph would be here, helping her with the boxes, and helping her, quietly, in his way, process each item. At moments like these, when she needed him, she missed him the most.

The one solace that April had, as she packed away Rose's stuff, was sleuthing, playing detective. It gave her some distance from the memories she associated with these objects. Mostly it was just a distraction from the pain.

At first. Then, as she dug further, the sleuthing became interesting. What she was discovering, as she sorted through Rose's stuff, was very interesting indeed. The more she sorted, the more she realized that she should have confronted her emotions and done this digging much earlier.

Everything seemed to offer some kind of lead. She found a diary that was full of disturbing nods and gestures toward April's worst fears. "Still not sure what to do about R," i.e., Ricky, Rose had written in one entry. "Feels like it's getting more dangerous." And in another: "Need to talk to R. Settle things. Need to convince him I'm not a threat to him. That I just wanna BE DONE with this and walk away."

On and on it went. Rose didn't always put a date on every entry, and April could sometimes only tell the entries apart from the different color pens she used. Often the details were hazy. Rose was always careful not to spell anything out too clearly, in case the diary ever fell into the wrong hands. Much of it probably would have been almost incoherent to somebody who didn't know Rose, her life, her way of speaking and thinking. But, of course, nobody on earth knew Rose better than her older sister, and so the meanings of these entries could not have been clearer to April. The police must have seen these diaries when they'd poked around Rose's stuff. And yet they'd never asked April about them. Another sign that they weren't doing their job well.

Rose had clearly been terrified of Ricky, and she'd gotten herself into something scary enough that she'd been afraid to speak about it even with April. She must have been afraid that in telling April what was going on, she'd endanger April, too. Rose had been trying to protect April from whatever it was that she knew about Ricky. April had suspected something like this had been going on . . . now here was the evidence, clear as day. Inevitably her thoughts turned to Joseph and the way he'd *insisted* that Ricky wasn't guilty. How could she have trusted Joseph for even a minute?

April continued flipping through the diary, gathering more evidence. She ripped out a few empty pages and began making her own notes, trying to make a clear timeline of events. In the days leading up to Rose's disappearance the diary entries got longer and more distressed. Rose had been getting more worried about Ricky. From these entries April could also tell that Rose hadn't seen or talked to Ricky in some time and that she was becoming more nervous that a meeting with him was necessary.

April put the book down for a moment and noticed something written on its inside cover. It was a long string of random letters and numbers—or, what anyone on earth would consider random. But, to April's eyes, they weren't random at all. It was a code that she and Rose had invented when they were kids.

They still used it, occasionally, sometimes to hide their thoughts from others, sometimes just for fun, in texts. The only two people on earth who could decipher this language were Rose and April. With only a tiny hesitation, April was able to decode the message. She translated the gibberish into:

Ri-Ri! if you're reading this because I'm IN TROUBLE—and that had better be the only reason you're reading it!—this is what you need to do right now. 1995_(my favorite cereal forever) at gmail. Password BabyElephant1995. It will tell you what you need to know.

For a quick second, April smiled. "Honey Smacks" had been Rose's favorite cereal when she was a kid. And BabyElephant was exactly the kind of password Rose would come up with. For one second, April felt happy; she felt, for a fleeting moment, that she had something of her sister, something that was really *her*. But that feeling only let her down, only reminded her of the sad and bitter fact that, actually, she didn't have her sister here. And might never again see her. But even that sadness didn't last. Now wasn't the time to linger on emotions. She'd done that for too long. No, April was on a mission. This was a huge lead. April sprang into action.

She grabbed her phone and immediately logged into the gmail account. The first e-mail was marked

as "Unread" and had the subject line: To April:
Please Read This First.

> *Dear Sis,*
> *If you're reading this, it means something bad*
> *has happened. But I guess you already know that.*
> *This is an encrypted account (fancy!)—that means*
> *any message I send from it is total anonymous, no*
> *trace of me on it at all. (Don't ask me how I did*
> *that.) Why did I create this account? 1) I needed*
> *a totally anonymous way to communicate with the*
> *police, if things got to that point. 2) I made a habit*
> *of erasing all of my e-mails with Ricky from my*
> *regular account—in case someone hacked it—*
> *and stored all of those messages here. I didn't*
> *want the wrong people to see them. And if anyone*
> *was gonna see them, I wanted that person to be*
> *you. I knew you'd know what to do with them. The*
> *reason I didn't tell you about this plan or this*
> *account is that I didn't want you to worry and I*
> *also didn't wanna put you in any kind of trouble.*
> *Don't be mad. Now that you're reading this, it*
> *means that trouble has already come. I'm so sorry,*
> *Ri-Ri. I've made some mistakes. I never wanted*
> *you to be mixed up in this.*
> *Love always,*
> *Rosie*

April suddenly remembered Rose referring to
this secret e-mail account. Once, when April had com-
plained to Rose that she needed to be more careful

about her communications, especially with Ricky, that she didn't know who was watching, she'd told April that she'd "set something up" and that she was taking every precaution possible.

As April read the archived e-mails, she got a clear and specific picture of the tense negotiations Rose had had with Ricky. "How can I trust you?" Rose wrote in one message. (And Ricky's reply: "You better start trying.") And in another message: "I don't feel safe seeing you alone. If we meet, we meet in public." At a certain point, after Ricky pleaded with her, Rose finally agreed to meet him. And after more tense negotiation, they agreed on the place, Finnegan's in North Philly, and on a day and time: July 9. A Thursday. 9 P.M.

April just stared at it.

A million thoughts rushed into her head. *July 9, July 9 . . . What was happening on that day?* Was that the last day Rose was seen? April scrolled into her own texts with Rose. The last text she'd received from her sister was two days earlier. July 7. April's eyes almost jumped out of her head: this meeting with Ricky on the 9th definitely happened during the same few days when Rose likely disappeared. April quickly scanned the rest of the e-mails in the inbox of this secret account. The last message, a message to Ricky, was dated also July 7. It was easy to imagine that Rose hadn't communicated with him after that—at least not by e-mail—and that they'd met on the 9th, and that was it.

And there was another glaring fact: This July 9th

meeting contradicted something Ricky had told April. When April had seen Ricky, when he'd shown up unexpectedly at the Metropolitan Bakery that night, he'd told her that the last time he'd seen Rose was *weeks* before she disappeared, when—according to him—Rose had come by his shop and broken up with him. But that was simply not true. She had the proof in this e-mail. Why was Ricky lying? What was he covering up?

Everything pointed in the same direction: Ricky. And if Ricky was, as she suspected, the person responsible . . . why had Joseph insisted that he was not? Why was he covering for Ricky? April collected all of Rose's diaries and put them into her bag. She knew what she needed to do.

Chapter Nine

April was busy now with a full-time job at the bakery and two stressful and time-consuming classes at the culinary school. But she spent every free second on her Rose investigations. She'd gone to Finnegan's, the bar where Rose and Ricky had been planning to meet on that night in July. She interviewed everyone who worked at the bar and who might have been there that night. She even tracked down some people who'd worked there but had left during the last few months. People seemed to remember both Ricky and Rose—both of whom were regulars at the bar—but nobody could place them at the bar on that particular night. If they had met, it wasn't the kind of meeting that made an impression on people: there wasn't a big fight or tears. Nobody got slapped. If anything of importance happened at that meeting, nobody at the bar seemed to know about it.

April had noticed that there were two security cameras in the bar: one mounted at the bar itself and one by the front door. But when April asked the security guy if they saved old footage, he told her, with regret, that they erased everything at the end of each week. If there was ever any footage of Ricky and Rose meeting, it had long since been erased. Everything seemed to be coming up empty.

But April wouldn't stop. Even while she was at work at the bakery or in class, April would review all the details in her mind, over and over again, looking for something she'd missed. She was doing that one night at the bakery, going over the details again in her head, just before closing time. She'd scrubbed down the tables and had retreated into the kitchen to begin putting away and cleaning everything there, and prepping the space for the next morning, when she heard a familiar voice from behind her.

"Hey," it said.

April froze. She took a deep breath.

Just breathe, she whispered to herself.

This was what she'd been preparing for during the past weeks, ever since she'd seen Rose's secret e-mails. But she hadn't thought it was actually going to happen, and certainly not that night, in the bakery as she closed up shop. But it was happening. Right now. A strange calmness came over her. She slipped her hand into the little purse she kept slung over her shoulder for just this reason, and turned around, pointing a .22 caliber Smith & Wesson pistol directly at Ricky's heart.

She held her arm extended, just slightly bent, with

her left hand gripping the shooting wrist, steadying it. She squared her eyes right behind the gun, to aim, just as she'd been practicing at a shooting range every day that week.

She'd bought the gun last week from a friend of one of her exes. She'd gone to the bar that he owned. She'd marched right in, sat at the bar, resisting the deep temptation to order a drink, and asked him if he'd sell her a gun. He sold her one that night, no questions asked.

"Hands up, Ricky. Right now. Higher."

Ricky lifted his hands in the air. He looked like he'd seen a ghost. April quickly approached him, keeping the gun squarely aimed.

"Keep them up," she said. "I swear to God I'll pull this trigger if you do anything. I would *love* to do it, Ricky. Do *not* tempt me. . . ."

With the gun in her right hand still pointed at him, she quickly reached into his belt, grabbed his gun, retreated to her position by the sink. She slipped his gun into her purse.

April could tell that Ricky was watching her in disbelief.

"Been practicing," she said.

"I can tell," he said. "Can I put my hands down now?"

"Yeah, put your hands down," she said. "I was gonna visit you, you know. But I'm glad you came here. We need to talk."

"Thank you. Could you stop pointing that thing at me?"

"I'll put it down when I feel like it. I'm gonna ask the questions here, okay? You gimme the answers. Got it?"

"Yeah."

"Yeah, *what?*" April said, clicking off the gun's safety.

"You ask the questions," Ricky said, nervously. "I give the answers. Got it."

"Ricky, I'm serious here. I know what you did. I will kill you right now, *happily*. Don't give me a reason. Now answer me: When and where was the last time you saw Rose?"

"She came by the shop. . . ."

"You're lying. I know you're lying."

"I'm not. I'm telling you . . ."

"I'm giving you a chance to make this right and to save yourself. I know the truth. I know everything, Ricky. So let's start from the beginning. Where was the last time you saw Rose *before* she supposedly disappeared?"

"I'm telling you," Ricky said now, more desperately, "it was when she came by my shop. . . ."

"SHUT *UP!*" April shouted. "I will pull this trigger. . . ."

"April, I swear, I swear that's what happened. . . ."

"I will KILL you if you continue lying. Tell me the truth and I'll spare you. It's the only way."

April was beginning to lose control of her rage.

Her hand, holding the gun, was beginning to tremble. And, in this sudden surge of emotions, she saw something in Ricky's face that unnerved her even more. He was terrified. No, it was worse: he was confused.

And his confusion was genuine. This wasn't the face of someone who was defiantly hiding information; it was the face of someone who was about to be executed and didn't have any clue what the executioner wanted from him. It wasn't what April expected to see and it terrified her. Why didn't he just tell her the truth, especially because his life depended on it? For the first time it occurred to April that he might not be lying. And yet . . . if he was, would she really kill him? Could she really pull that trigger? Her rage was strongly urging her to do it, to squeeze. And yet, that look in his face, that look . . .

"Okay. You have three choices here, Ricky," April said, in as calm a voice as she could.

"You tell me where Rose is *right* now—and you tell me when and where you're gonna let her go. If you do that, we're good. No trouble from me. You go your way, I go mine. Got it?"

"Yes," said Ricky.

"Or second choice: You *pretend* to tell me where she is, and tell me you're gonna let her go but *don't*: I will go to the cops and tell them everything. The pill smuggling business, the money laundering, the blackmail, the cover-ups, the weapons stuff, all of the assaults. Not to mention this kidnapping. EVERYTHING, Ricky."

Ricky looked at her in horror.

"You try to play me, I will testify against you in court. And, in case you can't tell, I'm gonna be a killer witness. And if you think you can scare me out of it, or kill me first, I'm telling you right now, and listen closely to what I'm saying: I've *already* written up my testimony, in detail, with dates and everything, and it's saved and backed up online in two separate places—in places where the police *will* find it if something happens to me. You can't and won't stop me from testifying. I will ruin you and put you in jail for the rest of your life. So better just play along with me. Got it? *Got it?*"

"Got it."

"And third option: You continue lying to me here, and I will put a bullet in you right now. Don't think I won't do it, Ricky. I got the gun for this reason. I've been picturing this for a while. I will kill you right here for what you've done. Got it?"

"Got it."

"Good. Now answer me: Where were you on the night of July 9?"

"What? Um, um. I'm not sure. That was a long time ago. I'd have to think about it."

"JULY NINTH! Where. Were. You?" April was shouting, her shooting hand now violently shaking.

"April, please, hold on. I really don't know. I'm

not lying. I don't know what you're talking about. I don't remember anything about that day. . . ."

"Ricky, I know you met my sister at Finnegan's! You said you last saw her at your shop. Well, I know that you saw her at least one other time, at Finnegan's . . ."

"No," he said. "No, no . . ."

"Actually, yes," April said. "I know you did. I saw the e-mail, Ricky. I saw the security tape"—she lied—"and I saw you two there on the recording. *Don't* lie."

Though April was terribly worked up now, she still had enough of her wits about her to tell that there was someone else now in the shop. Someone had come through the front door. She could hear footsteps. She immediately slipped the gun into her purse, just as a police officer appeared in the doorway.

"Everything okay in here?" he said.

Ricky just stared, but April, though struggling hard to rein in her agitation, smiled, trying to turn on the charm. "Oh, everything is *fine*, Officer. Thank you."

The cop gave a look around the space, and finally lingered on Ricky, giving him a long, suspicious glance that was intended as much to inspect him for any signs of wrongdoing as it was to communicate to Ricky that he was *Being Watched*.

"Do you know why I'm here?" the cop said, still looking at Ricky.

Ricky said nothing, but started making some sounds, as though he were about to mutter something. Again, April took the lead.

"It was my bad, Officer. I was getting a bit emotional. . . ."

"I heard shouting," the cop said.

"I know, I know. I'm sorry. Everything is okay here. Really."

"You work here?" he said to April.

She nodded, and pointed to her Metropolitan Bakery apron.

"You?" the cop said to Ricky. "You work here?"

"No, sir," Ricky muttered, his eyes fixed on the wall next to the officer.

"You want him out of here?" the cop said to April.

April hesitated, unsure what was best to say in this moment. Of course she wanted him to stay, so that she could finish her interrogation of him. But maybe that would be impossible now.

Ricky's eyes shot up.

"I should leave," he said.

"Good idea," said the cop. "And watch yourself."

Ricky turned around and left without a word. Now it was just the cop and April. She became suddenly aware of her purse, with two guns in it, neither of which she was licensed to carry. The cop leaned out the door, to make sure Ricky was away.

"Okay, he's gone. Anything you wanna tell me?"

There was so much she wanted to say. But she'd already tried with the police, and it had taken her nowhere.

"No," she said. "I was just letting off some steam. Just being a drama queen."

The cop smiled in a way that made April regret saying that. But, of course, it worked.

"All right, hon, you ever need anything—*anything*—you give me a shout." He leaned over and handed April his card. As she took it, he gently stroked her hand. She shuddered. And then he was gone.

Culinary school classes were harder than April expected. She wasn't at the top of her class—and she suspected that the people at the top didn't have full-time jobs, as she did. But she was keeping up, and even slowly progressing. By the end of the classes, which met three times a week for four-hour sessions, she was physically exhausted from all of the running around, the chopping and mixing, the lifting of heavy equipment and containers, and especially the mental stress of following orders, quickly, from unfriendly instructors, and enduring the nasty looks of competitive fellow students. She would walk home from these sessions in a fog, barely mustering the mental strength to guide her legs where they needed to go, and aching to collapse into her bed.

Which was why she missed the signs. The footsteps, the man walking too closely behind her. Until it was too late. It all happened quickly. The moment she turned a corner, onto a small street, the man pounced. From behind. With one quick motion. He struck a blow to her head, then grabbed her under her arms and hoisted her, almost threw her into a nearby alley. If he wasn't a professional, he was certainly someone who'd done this before, who knew what he was doing. He had chosen this corner, this alley beforehand. It had all gone down according to a careful plan.

Not that April didn't fight back. She did. She was exhausted and distracted from class but a rush of adrenaline coursed through her body and she felt strong and resilient and was scrambling as hard as she could. She was caught entirely by surprise at that moment, but she'd also been preparing for combat during the past few weeks. And there was the gun. It was in her purse. Even as she struggled to her knees, trying to steady herself—and to see where the attacker was: he seemed perpetually behind her, no matter where she turned. But the purse, she could see clearly, was lying about two feet away from her, on the ground where it had flown during the initial attack.

Without a single hesitation she lunged after it.

The kick was swift and it connected squarely with her ribs, sending her flying and flailing, out of control, until her body and head slammed with force into a Dumpster. And before she knew it, she was on the ground. Flat. Her cheek on the pavement. She felt sharp burning sensations all over. She couldn't move at all. In her fog, she heard someone take a deep breath. And then footsteps.

April was conscious enough to know that she was in serious trouble but too weak to do anything about it. It was as if some giant weight were bearing down on her. With her face pressed heavily against the pavement she had a view of the man's large white sneakers, and she studied them carefully, trying to commit their details to memory, in case . . . in case she survived this ordeal. And what were those sneakers doing? They seemed to be just standing there, and April got the sudden feeling that the man was looking at her.

Suddenly he shifted. Before she saw the sneakers move she could hear them: she could hear the sound of them rubbing over the loose pavement, over the grimy papers, the metal shards, and the broken glass. There was no question about it: his feet were making their way to her. April struggled desperately to move and felt a sudden electric bolt of pain in her ribs, and immediately collapsed. All she could do was brace her head for the blow she knew was coming.

She closed her eyes.

A sudden flurry of footsteps. A loud groan. And then the hard thud of a body slamming to the ground next to her. She cried out in pain. But realized that the pain she felt was still the pain of her ribs, from before. April opened her eyes and saw the man. He was facedown, like her, on the ground, but he was unconscious, his eyes closed curiously, almost peacefully, as though he were just taking a nap. April's mind didn't feel right; nothing was making sense.

With her waning strength, she tried to crane her head up, to see what was happening, to gain some ounce of clarity. And what she saw only confirmed that her mind was not right.

Joseph. It was him, standing there.

Was she imagining it? It was *someone,* some man. With city streetlights behind this person, he appeared almost like a shadow. But just from the shadow, the silhouetted form of this person, April could tell that it was Joseph. She knew that form well, had memorized its strong, expansive contours. He was holding a long tool of some kind. Was he coming after her? She was terribly confused.

"Jos—" she said, meekly.

He stepped closer to her and knelt down.

"Joe . . ." she said.

"*Shhhh,*" Joseph said, and put his hand on her forehead. "You're safe."

April saw that there was another man standing behind Joseph with his arms crossed. Her strength was ebbing. But she tried to make out who it was. When his face came into focus, April suddenly felt a wave of panic. It was Ricky. Just standing there.

April was done. She had no more energy. Everything went black.

Chapter Ten

April's eyes flashed open. A moment of panic swept over her. She had no idea where she was. She had no idea how she'd gotten wherever it was she was, nor any idea where she'd been. For a brief moment she thought maybe she was waking up from a long, long sleep, in which the disappearance of her sister, her relationship with Joseph and Carmen, and all the rest of it, had just been a wild dream.

But now, she was definitely awake. Only, where was she? This wasn't her room. She looked, with utter confusion, at the old-fashioned lace curtains at the window and the goofy dog-themed art on the wall. When had she gone to sleep? She certainly did not feel rested. She felt that her body was broken in every way. The moment her eyes flashed open, a wave of confusion immediately washed over her, her body shuddered, and she tried to sit up. But a shooting pain in her back and legs flattened her body. It was so pure and electric, it almost didn't hurt so much as simply grasp complete control over her movements.

"Whoa. Hey," she heard a man's voice suddenly say. "Just relax there."

It was a familiar voice. But nothing, not even her own body, felt familiar at the moment. April turned her head, carefully, trying not to trigger that electric pain again. The panic returned. It was Ricky. He was standing beside the bed, on a chair, messing with the curtain over the window.

"Uh, I'm just fixing this thing here," he said.

"No, no," she said. "What are *you* doing here . . . ?"

"It's okay, April," another voice said.

April saw Joseph walking through the door. Before she could protest, he'd put his hand on her forehead, which, despite her misgivings, gave her a measure of comfort.

"You're safe here," he said, whispering in her ear.

But his words only re-triggered April's confusion and sense of panic.

Her vision was clearing up. She could see that she was indeed lying in a bed, and that this bed was definitely not hers. But she was clearly in a woman's bedroom. Dim, late-afternoon sunlight was streaming in through lace-trimmed curtains. The place felt vaguely familiar.

"Where am I?" April finally said, realizing how dry her throat was and what a bad headache she had. She could feel her body shift, painfully, as someone sat down next to her on the edge of the bed.

"You're in my home, dear," Carmen said, handing April a tall glass of water. "Drink this down. You're safe here. I promise."

The sight of Carmen did finally put April at ease. She breathed easily at last. But now, as her mind was clearing, her questions only became more demanding.

"Why is *he* here?" April said, sitting up, carefully, looking toward Ricky. She took a giant drink of water, finishing the glass in one gulp. Just as Ricky was about to reply, Joseph raised his hand, stopping him.

"Please don't be upset, April," Joseph said. "He's with us now. He's okay. You gotta trust me."

April turned to Carmen, who nodded, and said, "It's true, hon. We'll explain everything. You need to trust us. We're all on the same team now."

April didn't reply at first.

"We're trying to figure out the next step," Joseph said.

"We?" April said, glancing toward Joseph. He didn't reply.

April sighed deeply and shut her eyes. She dropped her head back onto the pillow. She was already exhausted from this conversation.

"You just rest now, dear," Carmen said, taking April's hand. "We'll explain later."

"No," April said. "I need to know now. What's going on here?"

"Okay," Joseph said, sitting down again, and smoothing the creases out of his pants, a gesture that was so familiar to April. "I'll tell you everything we know."

* * *

"Someone has been following you around," Joseph began.

April glanced over at Ricky, her eyes narrowed.

"You're right, April," Joseph continued. "It was one of Ricky's guys. But he was following you around to watch over you. To *protect* you. He was the one who called me when you were attacked. He actually was the one who saved you."

"From who?"

Joseph hesitated.

"Tell her," Carmen said. "Just tell her."

"From an incredibly dangerous man named Gabriel Hornung," Joseph said. "But most people call him Whitey."

Joseph paused for a moment to let April absorb this new information.

"Those were the guys who broke into your apartment, April," Joseph said. "That was the guy who left Rose's sweater in your freezer that night. With the note telling you to stop searching for Rose. That was Whitey's people."

April said nothing. Her eyes remained shut to conserve energy.

"Joseph is telling the truth," Carmen said. "So is Ricky."

"Why?" April turned weakly toward Ricky. "Why were you trying to keep me off the trail?"

"It was for your own good," Joseph cut in. "And for Rose's, too."

"How do *you* know that, Joe?"

Joseph told her that he'd suspected it for a while—

and finally Ricky himself had convinced him. And he got confirmation from Lemuel, that shady guy they'd met in the woods that day, the guy who'd worked with Ricky. This Lemuel had also just been brutally assaulted—just days before April had been attacked. Lemuel, too, was ambushed by assailants sent by the same guy: Whitey. But Lemuel hadn't been as lucky as April. His wounds proved to be fatal.

But before he died, Joseph rushed to visit him in the hospital, and asked him what he knew. And that's when Joseph finally learned the whole story. The person who was holding Rose was indeed the notorious Whitey Hornung. This was what Ricky had been trying to tell Joseph, and what Lemuel himself had been hinting when they'd met in the woods—but now he was ready to confirm it.

Earlier, when Joseph and April had met at Lemuel's cabin in the woods, Lemuel hadn't wanted to tell them this piece of information directly. He, like everyone—including Ricky—was terrified of Whitey. All he was willing to reveal at that meeting was that the kidnapper *wasn't* Ricky. But now, on his deathbed, he could tell the whole truth: Whitey, the notorious formerly Amish gangster, was the man behind everything. It was, in fact, this bit of information—that Lemuel knew who'd kidnapped Rose—that got him killed. Whitey's men had likely discovered him talking to April and Joseph. And this conversation, too, was the reason that Whitey finally struck at April: he assumed that she knew everything, and so she had to go, too.

April closed her eyes, trying to process all of this information. Her head hurt, and she was in a fog. She kept her eyes shut long enough that Joseph assumed she'd fallen back asleep. "Let's give her some space," he said.

"No," April said. "I'm awake. Keep going. Fine. So Ricky wasn't the one. This Whitey guy was. But tell me *why*, Joseph. Why did Whitey choose Rose?"

Joseph sighed deeply.

"Well," he said, "that's where Ricky comes in."

April's eyes shot open. She turned to Ricky and gave him a long menacing look. He just looked away.

At first, Whitey had kidnapped Rose as part of a plan to extort Ricky, Joseph said. Whitey was a skilled gangster and he'd worked out the following scheme: he had a business extorting lower-level gangsters. The racket was simple. If Ricky wanted to run his drug smuggling operation, which was on Whitey's turf, he had to pay Whitey for protection; and once this drug business grew and became very profitable, Whitey would up the price, significantly. He would demand a much higher price. Or else. That was just business as usual for Whitey.

Ricky had refused. At first. Really, he was bluffing, intending to buy some time so that he could think things over and figure out how to get that kind of money. But Whitey wasn't having it. He was not a patient man. And worse: Whitey was not just a shrewd businessman he was also a sadist. He liked the power plays, he enjoyed inflicting pain and violence. So Whitey struck back, without warning. He had his men beat Ricky up. Bad. And they left a message with Ricky: until you pay off the debt, your beloved Rose will be in Whitey's hands. You try to run, or do anything, Rose pays. At that point, Rose was simply being held as collateral in this extortion plot. As soon as Ricky paid up, Whitey would return her home, he said.

"I knew it was your fault," April hissed at Ricky.

"I didn't know he would do that," Ricky said, suddenly emotional. "I never wanted Rose to get caught up in this. I've been trying to get her back."

Joseph continued. Things got worse. The situation changed dramatically when Whitey learned Rose's identity. Whitey's spies discovered an interesting fact about his captive: as Whitey's men were busy trying to stop April in her search, they discovered that this sister of Rose was dating an Amish guy, one Joseph Young. They immediately reported this back to Whitey. When he heard it, his ears perked up. Was this Joseph Young . . . the son of Hezekiah Jonathan Young? His spies confirmed that, yes, he was *that* Joseph Young.

This changed everything for Whitey. Hezekiah Jonathan Young, Joseph's father, was Whitey's older brother. And a nemesis of his. (Whitey had long ago changed his name to Hornung, another family name, in order to distance himself from the family he despised.) Now that it turned out this Rose girl in his possession was connected to the Youngs—his own estranged family—the situation turned from business transaction to personal vendetta.

Whitey immediately reneged on his offer to return Rose when Ricky paid up. No, the price for Rose immediately climbed higher. Much, much higher.

"Ricky?" Joseph now said. "Do you want to explain to April what Whitey told you?"

"Yeah, okay," Ricky said. "I went to pay him. You know, to pay up? It was a lot of money. More than I had. But I paid. But then one of Whitey's guys says to me, 'Whitey thanks you for the money but he wants you to know that Rose stays with him.' Those were his words."

April was silent. Now Carmen spoke.

"What did you do next, Ricky?" Carmen asked. "When that happened?"

"I flipped out, completely flipped out," Ricky said, and turned to face April. "That's why I came around to your shop, to the bakery, April. And then you pulled the piece."

Carmen's eyes bulged. She turned to April.

"You were carrying *a gun* in the bakery? You pulled it out!"

April was too tired to explain or even to register a reaction on her face.

"Sorry," she muttered to Carmen. "I wanted to tell you. But didn't want you to worry."

"Well, it's okay, hon," Carmen said, trying to put on a brave face. "The fact is, you were right to be scared. If I had any idea that *that man* was behind this . . ." Carmen just shook her head, scared to even finish the thought. "You have no idea who this

Whitey is, April. But *I* do, 'cause I grew up Amish. And Joseph knows, too," Carmen said, pointing at Joseph.

He nodded.

"It's true," he said. "Everyone in our community knows that guy," Joseph said. "And I'm kin. So I know better than most. He's evil, April. *Real* evil."

"Yeah," Ricky jumped in. "And where I do business . . . we know all about him, too. Nobody messes with that guy."

"That's why I was so nervous and didn't tell you," Joseph said to April. "I was afraid you might do something like try to find Whitey or something. I did not want you going near him. But I was getting information. That Rose's disappearance was connected to Whitey. But I didn't want to tell you that, or what it meant. Because I didn't want to scare you or lead you into trouble. I just kept trying to figure it out myself and, in the meantime, to protect you from it. But I was always, *always*, even when we . . . broke up, I was always keeping an eye on you, April. And searching for Rose."

April's eyes suddenly found Joseph's. A familiar feeling passed between them. Oh, familiar eyes! Those eyes that felt to her like a warm home.

April hadn't looked into those eyes since she'd been attacked. In fact, it had been much longer than that. She hadn't looked into those eyes for weeks. They'd broken up. He'd stopped coming around to the bakery, to give her space when she was at work with Carmen.

Of course, April's real work was to not fall apart, and to grasp on to what remained of her breaking heart. She was in culinary school; she was fresh off probation; she was in search of her missing sister. April needed to keep it together. And so they'd stopped seeing each other. But until they were actually apart, she hadn't realized how much she'd come to rely on those eyes, on the sense of safety and love that emanated from them. And now, unexpectedly, here they were again. She was right next to Joseph. But, even so, she hadn't dared look into his eyes until he'd said those words:

I was always keeping an eye on you, April.

And immediately her eyes, out of pure instinct, went searching for his again. Joseph's eyes: her home. The only home she'd ever known.

It was a powerful moment of reunion between April and Joseph. But it was just a moment. They were broken up. And there were good reasons for that. Reasons that still applied. And there were more urgent needs at the moment: April and Joseph knew that neither their love, nor their breakup, was a topic for discussion at the moment. There was too much work to do. Rose was out there, after all. She was alive, it seemed. But she was in grave danger. That was all that mattered right now.

April looked away from Joseph. And Joseph, too, caught himself, and looked away. Carmen saw this, saw the entire exchange between April and Joseph, and she quickly jumped in.

"Guys? Right now? We need to talk about Whitey," she said. Joseph nodded. April just closed her eyes.

"Tell her," Carmen said to Joseph. "Go ahead. Tell her who Whitey is."

"Remember that story I told you?" Joseph said to April. "In your apartment? Remember you asked me to tell you a ghost story? And I did. Remember it?"

How could she forget? Joseph had told her that it was a true story. The boy in that story was traumatized when his sister was accidentally buried alive. That boy never believed that she was dead. And he'd lingered by the graveside until he'd heard sounds coming from inside. He was the one who'd set off the alarm that night and gotten the family to start digging, to rescue his sister. She'd come out alive, but she was never the same. Nobody was, really. That little boy blamed his family for the monstrous accident.

"That little boy was Whitey," Joseph said. "He never forgave his family. *My* family."

And now that boy, all grown up, had become a dangerous gangster and cult leader, notorious for his brutal tactics.

"Whitey is your . . . uncle?" April said. "You didn't mention that."

"I don't think of him that way," said Joseph. "But yes, he is."

Whitey continued to pretend to stay within the Amish fold even though he was actually shunned by the community. But they lived in fear of him. And he used the Amish way of life as one of his covers for his criminal enterprises. He'd also, they said, created a small cult, in which he used the trappings of Amish life to lure unsuspecting followers. The cult he'd created wasn't about business but about his sick need for adoration. Most people speculated that it was the result of his trauma from childhood. Whatever it was, his staying close to the community kept his enemies, and his siblings, on edge constantly. Meanwhile, from his compound in Amish country, his power grew and grew.

And with Rose, who'd fallen into his net almost by chance, Whitey saw a chance to exact vengeance on the Young family, it seemed. And yet . . . what *did* he really want with Rose? Was it about money? Whitey always wanted money. But, oddly, it didn't appear to be his motive in this case.

"Well," April said, "what *are* his demands then? What does he want?"

Joseph and Ricky exchanged a look.

"*What* is it?" April said. "Just tell me."

"We, um," said Joseph. "We don't . . . we don't know."

"He didn't say?" April asked.

"We can't get him to say," Ricky said.

"Tell me what this means," April insisted, using all her strength to sit up, and look back and forth between Ricky and Joseph. "What are you guys not telling me?"

"There's nothing we're not telling you," Joseph

said. "That's the problem. He didn't say anything about his demands. He isn't making them. He's not responding to us at all. And we don't know what that means."

"Why can't we go to the police with this?" April asked.

Another look between Joseph and Ricky.

"That's what makes Whitey so dangerous," Joseph replied. "He works with the police. Gives them information. And they stay out of his way."

"He works as an FBI informant," Ricky clarified. "You know, a snitch for the feds."

"How do you know that?" April said.

Joseph looked at Ricky.

"We know," Ricky said. "He talks to them all the time. One time, we set up a trap. We had someone tell him some made-up stories and then we heard—don't ask me how, we have ways—we heard that the feds were talking about these BS stories. And they could only have gotten them from Whitey. That's when we learned that he plays it both ways. But, really, we already knew it. That's why we set up the trap in the first place."

Since the FBI considered Whitey a valuable asset, he operated under privileges. There was also reason to believe that some corrupt elements within the Bureau were themselves getting rich working with him, and so they had an added incentive to keep him out of legal trouble. Any time local or even state police would begin to close in on Whitey for something, the FBI would step in and find ways to get them to back off. Which meant that nobody dared cross Whitey because he worked under federal protection. And Whitey, without a leash, was a dangerous wild animal.

"Is this why the cops have been so useless with Rose?" April asked.

"That's what I'd guess," Ricky said. "Cops ain't gonna do nothing here. If anything, they're gonna try to shut us down. If Rose has a shot, we gotta do this ourselves."

Chapter Eleven

Two women walked down the long hallway, arms folded. They said not a word. The only sound that was heard was the tapping and echoing of their heels against concrete. All of this was intentional. Whitey had many rules and regulations. *Laws,* he called them. And he was strict about them. In the Compound—which he'd designed himself, and which he'd spent nearly a decade constructing—he'd built unusually long halls, made of poured concrete. The idea was to create an intimidating environment. The women of Whitey's group—all eleven of them, most of them runaways, some of them Amish runaways—were called the Community. The members of the Community were required to wear a certain shoe with metal heels that would make a maximum of sound as they walked around. And the women weren't permitted to speak in the halls. As he told the women, "I want you to be alone. Alone with the sound of your footfalls."

The Community had many such laws. All members of the Community were to refer to Whitey as

"Bishop," as in "yes, Bishop" and "thank you, Bishop." Every piece of clothing was mandated by the Bishop. The women had to keep a notebook in which they recorded their thoughts. Every morning, when they awoke, they were to record the dreams they'd had the night before and show these reports to Whitey.

Whitey harshly upheld the Laws. But it was rare that he had to: he had other means of persuasion at his disposal. It wasn't terror that kept the women obedient. Whitey manipulated their minds, their wills. Occasionally one of the women would wake up from this brainwashing and challenge him, but it was rare. Increasingly rare, in fact, since Whitey, over the years, had become more skilled.

In the main chamber of the Compound, where Whitey held court, the women could speak only when spoken to. In their own rooms, which they shared, two to a room, they could speak openly. But they knew—or, at least those who'd been around long enough knew—that Whitey was always listening. And watching. And those who didn't know that, usually those who were new to the Community, would soon find out. There were other things— secrets—that new members of the Community would soon learn. But not right away.

The two newest members of the Community arrived on a Sabbath morning. It was mid-summer and the foliage was thick, covering the Compound heavily, blocking out much of the sun. This deep in the woods, the Compound was hardly visible in the trees. The two new members of the Community were walking down the long hall, arms crossed, as they'd been instructed by Grand Martha—Whitey's deputy, a solemn woman whose hair fell all the way down her back, and who never smiled. These two women walked, their footsteps echoing loudly on the concrete floor, not saying a word.

Today would be their first rite. They didn't know what to expect. Grand Martha had been vague about it, just as she was vague about everything. But they had complete faith in Whitey. It was that faith, after all, that had brought them here to begin with. And it was a faith that Whitey had masterfully cultivated once they'd joined.

As they walked the long hall, and heard their loud footsteps, they followed Whitey's training: to mentally focus on the sound of those footsteps, to let all thoughts disappear. To not think at all. But to just listen. To follow the echo of the footsteps. To, as Whitey said, "keep following the echo, until the next echo, and the next . . ." for many minutes—for far longer than they expected—and to repeat, to no end, this mantra, under their breath: *Kudsha brikh-hu, Kudsha brikh-hu, Kudsha brikh-hu . . .*

Which means, in Aramaic, *The Holy One, Blessed is He*. Repeated over and over again. Until the sound on their lips, the sound of their feet on the concrete, and all of the echoes within echoes, mingled into one swirling spell, putting their heads into a kind of trance.

By the time they reached the main chamber, they were nearly hypnotized. And then they entered. They sat and swayed, with their heads spinning in ecstatic circles of *Kudsha brikh-hu, Kudsha brikh-hu, Kudsha brikh-hu.* And Whitey spoke to them in a loud whispering voice. It was a strange effect: he spoke to them as a group but, because it was a whisper, his words entered into every single woman's ear as though it really were a secret just for her to know.

The entire Community was there, that day, in the chamber. Eleven women, now thirteen, arranged in two small concentric circles. The inner circle was for higher-ranked members, the outer circle was for novices. They sat, cross-legged on mats. Sometimes Whitey would tell them to stand, or to adopt a pose and hold it while he spoke. Sometimes he would command them to lie on their backs, prone, with their eyes closed, as he spoke, telling them stories, giving them instructions, or rebuking them. Sometimes he would speak in Aramaic. Or he would lead them in hours of meditation until they were in an even deeper trance. He would hand out special concoctions for them to drink. An aid, he said, in their prophetic experience.

Whitey himself usually sat on a mat placed at the center of the circle. Though often he would walk around the outside of the circle, sometimes letting a hand come to rest on a woman's shoulder or back, sometimes whispering private messages into their ears as he walked by.

On this day, when the two new novices of the Community entered the chamber—already somewhat hypnotized—they found the other women seated on their mats. In the center of the circle, seated above them, in a chair, was a young woman in a white dress, wearing a bonnet that was stitched with a veil that completely covered her face. Her hair flowed wildly out of the bonnet, almost down to her shoulders. Her hands were tied with bright red ribbons, to the sides of the chair. But she made no effort to loosen these bonds. In fact, she barely moved at all.

"Yes, yes, enter," said the man's voice as the two novices opened the door and stood by it.

"Please take your places," the voice said.

It was Whitey, of course.

In a far corner of the room, he suddenly appeared; he'd been almost invisible standing against the wall in his all-white clothing. Now he slowly walked toward the circle of women sitting on their mats. His arm was extended, showing the new women the way to their own mats, which were waiting for them at the edge of the circle.

"Welcome," he said, "please make yourselves comfortable. This is *your* home."

When he said this, all the women—already trained in Whitey's program—sighed loudly in unison, and said, together, "*Our* home."

Whitey smiled congenially at the new members, and said, "See?"

One of the new members glanced, for just a moment, at the young woman who was seated in a chair in the middle of the circle, her hands bound, her face masked. She could see that the bound woman had reacted in some way to those words *our home*. But it wasn't clear what that reaction was.

When all were seated, Whitey led the women in chanting and breathing exercises. All the while, the tied-up woman sat in the chair, barely moving. Occasionally her head would dip down, or fall back for a moment, as though she were falling asleep.

After a while, when Whitey felt his flock was sufficiently mesmerized, he said, "Lie on your backs, eyes closed." Which they did. And while they did, he disappeared for a moment. And then another moment. He was a master of these pauses, of creating drama.

Whitey reappeared, followed by another young woman, who was pushing a cart that held a big, steaming pot.

"Open your eyes," Whitey said, in a near whisper. "And sit up."

The women did as Whitey said.

He walked over to the girl who was bound to the chair in the middle of the room. He took out a knife that had been holstered on his belt, and he raised it for all to see.

El maleh rahamiiim! he shouted.

Adonai hu ha Elohim! the women shouted back in unison.

Whitey circled the knife over the girl's head twice. He could feel the eyes of women in the room, glued to him, watching carefully what he would do next to this mysterious prisoner, whom none of them had ever seen before.

Suddenly, and without warning, he shouted *Adonai hu ha Elohim!* and brought the knife down over the girl's bonnet, over the veil that covered her face, ripping it from side to side, so that the lower half of her face, her mouth, was exposed. But her eyes remained concealed.

One by one, the women walked over to the bound girl and bowed, then took a spoonful of the soup in the pot, and fed it to the girl; they gave her drinks of water from a jug, and whispered *you are loved,* and kissed her on the forehead.

Rose hadn't eaten in almost two days. And the soup, though plain, nourished her and gave her joy such as she couldn't remember feeling in all her life. When all the women had finished feeding her, Whitey petted her forehead gently and brushed her hair lovingly with his fingers. And he whispered, "Your ordeal is over. You're safe here. You're home." Rose, finally feeling a bit of energy, whispered, "Thank you" so quietly that Whitey couldn't hear her.

He leaned down toward her, and whispered, "What did you say, my darling?"

He leaned in close to her mouth, so that he could hear her better.

"I said," Rose whispered, "I said . . . *I love you.*"

* * *

Though her body was slow in mending, April regained her mental clarity within a few days. Even though she still needed to rest, and she only left Carmen's apartment infrequently and with great effort, she insisted on being included in every conversation and decision.

Joseph, Ricky, and Carmen had turned Carmen's apartment into a kind of headquarters where they carefully plotted their next moves. The alliance was, to say the least, uneasy. Ricky, more accustomed to criminal activity, had taken measures to sweep Carmen's apartment of any bugs, to ensure that there weren't any surveillance devices—and while he did that, April watched him carefully to make sure that *he* wasn't installing any surveillance devices.

She still didn't trust him. "How do we know he's not working for Whitey?" she whispered to Carmen when the men were away. The measures that Ricky was taking to avoid detection only unnerved her more. And Joseph and Carmen, too, were bothered by it: Ricky just seemed a bit too good at this kind of thing, a bit too professional, a bit too skilled at sneaking around, and it made all of them trust him less.

Ricky had a connection close to Whitey. Which meant that Ricky knew a bit about Whitey's movements and plans. This connection was willing to give them information, but that was all; he would offer them no other help.

All of this only made Joseph and Carmen more suspicious of Ricky: he just seemed too close to Whitey. How could they be sure he wasn't passing information about them to the gangster? Maybe he was playing all sides, too, just like Whitey. They were taking a gamble on Ricky. But what choice did they have? Ricky seemed to be their best bet. They needed his know-how. Eventually, they knew that they'd need his men, too, and their muscle. And after all, it was one of Ricky's guys who'd saved April's life. Unless, of course, that too had been a ruse to gain their trust.

At this point, Ricky's connection to Whitey offered them updates every few days, about Whitey and sometimes even something about Rose. It was the clearest indication that they had gotten in months about Rose's whereabouts, and her condition. It scared April to hear these updates, because they confirmed just how much danger Rose was in. She was truly in the hands of a sick and dangerous man, a person capable of anything. And yet these concrete pictures of her sister also gave her hope that she was alive. That she was even close by. It was better than the other option.

Based on the updates they were getting about Whitey—his movements, and even his moods—the team of Ricky, Joseph, Carmen, and April were trying to get a picture of Whitey's operations, especially its patterns: what were his daily routines and what were the potential weak spots in his operation? They were trying to determine where and when and how they might be able to strike at Whitey and either free Rose directly or else gain enough leverage against Whitey that they could negotiate her freedom.

They kept lists and made charts of any information they gathered on Whitey. On the walls of Carmen's apartment they posted a picture of Whitey, along with photos of everyone attached to him, and created a web of connections that they could see and consult in order to understand how best to get closer to Whitey, or better yet, slip through his defenses, and grab Rose. The goal was clear enough: they needed to infiltrate Whitey's world and release Rose.

At the end of every day, they studied their options and tried to gather more intelligence. They did this for weeks. They did it for a month. Every day they got a clearer picture of how Whitey worked. Who were his second- and third-in-command, what their weaknesses were. Based on all of the information, Carmen noticed that Whitey rarely left the Compound, but that his second-in-command left at least twice a week, sometimes more, to handle business in neighboring towns. They knew what car he drove. What diners he ate at.

"We should ambush him on the road," Carmen said. "Use him somehow. Maybe even use him to sneak into the Compound."

The plan was to learn as much as possible about this guy so that when they grabbed him, they could scare him with credible threats if he didn't help them.

"He's a family man," Ricky said with a grin. "Got a big family. Likes talking about them. We overheard him showing pictures of his nieces to a waitress at the diner he goes to. If we're looking for an angle, that's it."

"So . . . what are you proposing?" Carmen asked, hesitantly.

"We grab him on the road somewhere. Put a gun in his mouth. We show him pictures of his mom and his brothers, you know, his cute little nephews and nieces. We show him that we know their addresses. We show the dude photos we took of the kiddies, and that we've driven there and have a plan to take them out if he doesn't help us. Promise you this: he'll do anything we ask him."

"And what do we ask him to do for us?" April said.

They would ask him to help them sneak Rose out. They would put this plan into action immediately, before this guy had any chance to take precautions to protect his family, or to alert Whitey. Ricky and Joseph, both armed, would be with the guy the whole time, watching him. Making sure he was doing what they asked. They would show him a live Skype feed of Ricky's men, in position, ready to launch an assault against his family's house if he tried anything. They would go with him into the

Compound, hiding in his car—just to keep him honest.

He would get Rose in the middle of the night. And then drive them all out, to a predetermined spot. Whitey was always in bed by 9:00 P.M., and his apartment in the Compound was a sealed bunker: soundproof. Whitey never appeared at night. They knew this from their inside guy. The deal would be simple: deliver Rose and they would forget about everything. And if Whitey's man tried to renege on the deal, they would kill a niece or a nephew or maybe both. It was an aggressive plan but it seemed feasible.

Ricky looked at their charts sprawled out on the table.

"Looks from here," Ricky said, "like that dude's gonna leave the Compound in two days, maybe three. We get this plan going *right now,* we can be there, waiting for him."

"Are you all completely insane?" April said. "I don't like any of this. I'm not gonna kill some little kids."

"Don't worry," Ricky replied to her. "You won't. We'll take care of everything."

"Oh, will *we?*" April said, staring Ricky down. "And that makes it all right?"

"Honey," Carmen said to April. "Nobody is going to get killed. Nobody is even gonna get hurt. It's just a *threat,* you know, to make sure he does what we ask him to. And so he doesn't try anything on us. We got to fight hard here. But it's just a *bluff,*" Carmen said, turning and glaring at Ricky. "Isn't that right, Ricky?"

Ricky thought about this for a moment and replied, "Yeah, that's right. We convince him we're serious and he'll cave right away. You'll see."

"*Nobody will get hurt*," Carmen said. "And most important, we get Rose back."

Chapter Twelve

The plan was set. Ricky went into full battle mode. He drove around the roads himself, looking for the right spot to set up the ambush. And once he found it, he installed his men there, in shifts, waiting with clear directions from him. He gave them a three-step plan. The first step was to call him. He'd be staying in a motel nearby. In the meantime, he lurked around the home of Whitey's deputy, taking photos of the house, the kids playing outside in the yard. Once they got the guy, they'd bring him to the motel and shake him down and show him these pictures. Ricky had gathered all the necessary materials: the rope and tape. According to the information they'd gathered, Whitey's deputy was due for a trip out of the Compound. It couldn't be more than a couple of days. And it could be any minute. They were ready.

They waited and waited some more. A day passed. Nothing. Two days passed and nothing. Finally, there was some movement. But it wasn't what Ricky or anyone was expecting. And suddenly their carefully laid plan went out the window.

The call came into Carmen's phone early on a Sunday morning. Joseph, Carmen, and April were staying at a motel outside of Lancaster. A different place from where Ricky and his men were, but close enough to be helpful, if needed.

The call came in shortly after dawn. It was Ricky. Over the past two days, he'd been calling in with regular updates—always to say, *Nothing new, still waiting.* Even so, every time he called, everyone jumped. They were expecting big news any minute. So when the call came very early Sunday morning, Carmen, who was still in bed, grabbed the phone.

"What's new?" she said.

"Crazy, *crazy* things," Ricky replied. "I . . . don't even know."

He sounded flustered, out of breath. It sounded like he was running. Carmen could hear men shouting behind Ricky, and cars starting.

"Omigod, what is it?" Carmen said, quickly running to wake up April and Joseph.

"Get in your car *right now,*" Ricky said over the phone. "Go to this address."

"Okay, okay," Carmen said, shaking April and Joseph awake and mouthing "Get dressed" to them.

Ricky gave her the address. As she repeated it, and wrote it down, Joseph's eyes got wide.

"I know exactly where that is," he said, as he quickly buttoned his shirt. "It's an old family address."

"Ricky," Carmen said, "what is happening here?"

"You're not gonna believe me," he said. "Whitey sent me a message. He knew we were waiting for his guy. I don't know how. . . ."

April and Carmen exchanged a look.

"He wants us to know," Ricky continued, "that he's moving first."

"What does that mean, 'moving'?" Carmen said. "What did he *do?*"

"He buried Rose," Ricky said. "He buried her alive."

"What are you *saying?* Like actually buried, in the ground?"

"In the ground," Ricky said. "But alive. That's what he said. He buried her alive. And he gave us the address."

April, now almost fully dressed, had stopped tying her shoe. Her hands froze in panic.

"It's like he wants us to go there," Ricky said. "To dig her up. We're already on the way. We've got shovels. We'll be there before you. Go!"

"We're on our way," Carmen said, and threw her phone into her purse as they raced to her car.

In the car, even as they sped, April was strangely quiet. Carmen was driving, Joseph was giving directions. And, in the back seat, April just sat there, stunned.

"I'm calling an ambulance," she said quietly. And she did. And after she convinced the dispatcher that this wasn't a hoax, she hung up. And sat there stunned once again.

"Is this a trap?" she said, finally.

Nobody replied. It was what they were all thinking.

"Well," said Carmen, "it could be. But we have no choice. We have to take the risk."

"What are we gonna see there?" April said.

Nobody replied. But Joseph turned around and reached back and took April's hand in his.

When they finally got close to the address, April was squeezing his hand as hard as she could. And when they turned into the long driveway, Joseph leaned back toward her, held April's eyes with his, nourishing her with their warmth, and said, "April, we'll get through this. Whatever it is."

Then they arrived. The doors flew open and they catapulted themselves out of the car, toward the backyard, where Ricky and his men were already digging furiously.

They, too, fell on their knees and began to dig. Nobody said a word. They just dug.

After this first frenzy, April paused. She realized that she wasn't breathing. She'd burned through all of her adrenaline within seconds, and now her head was swimming.

Breathe, she told herself.

A strange feeling suddenly came over her. The

feeling that she was being watched. Maybe Joseph felt it, too. Or maybe he was just sensing her uneasiness, but he also stopped digging for a moment.

They looked at each other. Joseph didn't dare say what was on his mind. But April could sense it: *Whitey*. He was nearby. He must have been nearby— but how near? Maybe he was watching them. Maybe that was his plan.

It made sense, in the twisted way that Whitey's mind made sense of things. Why did he want them to come out here? Why had he given them such clear directions? Didn't kidnappers hold on to their captives? Didn't murderers want to hide their crimes? Whitey had literally invited them to the scene of it. What was he up to?

Joseph shook his head, as if to say, Don't think about *that*. And, to April's anxious gaze, he replied, "Don't, April. Forget him. You know what we gotta do. Let's just do it."

With that, they both turned back to the ground and continued digging.

Earlier that day, first thing that morning, Whitey had woken up Rose. When he'd first kidnapped her, he'd treated her the way he treated all of his captives.

But Whitey had taken a special liking to Rose. Even before he knew who she was, he'd found himself drawn to her. He'd gotten into the habit of waking her up himself, quietly unlocking her door so he could crouch next to her bed, watching her gently sleep.

She really did look like his beloved sister, he thought.

More and more, each day, he saw the resemblances between Rose and Hefsibah, the girl who was buried alive—the physical similarities were striking. The red hair in long curls, the big eyes, the slightly pouty lips. She *was* Hefsibah. God had brought her back and delivered her to him. And not only that: she was the Hefsibah he remembered so well—the one who was full of life, the Hefsibah *before the incident,* before the burial. Somehow, some way, God had brought back his older sister, whom he loved more than anyone, and restored blooming life to her.

That very morning, as on all recent mornings, Whitey slunk into her room at 4:30, before anyone else was up. He lit a small candle, gently brushed her hair back from her forehead with his fingers, and whispered, "*Hefsibah . . . it's time to wake up, sweetie.*"

He took her hand and squeezed it tightly. He kissed her on the forehead. Just as he did every morning.

Except this morning was different. She didn't know that—although, in his heart, Whitey suspected that she did know, that she knew everything. How could she not know? Her eyes were so wide and knowing. He believed that she knew everything that was to come. That she knew, as well, that it was all for the good. That it was necessary. Yes, Whitey believed that she approved of the ordained plan, of what he was bound to do. And her approval moved him deeply. Whitey was not a humble man. But he was genuinely humbled before what he truly believed was Rose's willing sacrifice.

"My brave, brave girl," he whispered that morning upon waking her. "What did I do to earn your love back?"

Whitey was in tears.

"Today is the day, my dear," he whispered as she opened her eyes that morning. The sight of her eyes closed, then opening, was almost too much for him to bear. Whitey turned away and wept for a moment. Then, gathering himself, he repeated to her, "Today is the day, my dear Hefsibah."

She hadn't replied right away. But then a tiny smile curled about her lips. "Thanks, Poppa," she whispered, groggily. "I was hoping you'd say that."

He'd held a ritual for her in the main sanctuary. He had her lie down on her back in the center of the circle. One after another, each member of the Community took a turn walking up to her, kneeling beside her, kissing both of her cheeks, and whispering into her ear, "Good-bye, Hefsibah, we will see you soon."

Every single woman was in tears; some sobbed openly. They had come to love the mysterious girl named Hefsibah. And they had been moved deeply to see how much this girl had, for reasons they could barely understand, captured the heart of their leader. His love for her was obvious. It was a love they all shared. They could also tell that there was something more, something deeply painful for Whitey behind this love, something that they would never understand. And so they wept for that, as well. When they saw her tears, it only opened up their hearts even more.

From this room full of tears, Whitey removed Rose for the last time. He gently bound her feet and hands with ribbons—*to keep you safe,* he whispered to her, and she nodded—blindfolded her, and carefully placed her in the back seat of his van. He drove her out to the site, near the creek, near his old family's house—which he'd purchased and kept empty, as a sacred ground. This was where his sister had been buried that first time. He sang the hymns that had so moved his sister as a child. He looked in his rearview mirror and saw the blindfolded girl, her hair hanging messily over her face, just sitting still, listening to him.

"Sing with me," he said. And she did.

After spending so much time with Whitey, Rose knew the words to "I'll Fly Away." And they were beautiful to her.

Whitey remembered seeing his sister's body laid out, dead—or so everyone had said. They were preparing her for burial. He hadn't thought about that image for many years. But now, as he was driving to bury Rose, it came back to him as vividly as the day it had happened. Her hair had been tied back in braids. She was wearing a Sunday dress. Her arms had been folded over her chest, her favorite bonnet folded in her hands, her eyes, gently closed. Even to Whitey, who was younger, she had looked so small, so slight. Gone was the energizing force that had given her life.

But it was she. Hefsibah was right there. And young Whitey had refused to accept his family's insistent claim that she was dead. Finally, when his father had lost patience with Whitey and said, *Enough foolishness,* his sadness and frustration had come together into something else: rage. It had suddenly and horrifyingly occurred to him that his father was deceiving him intentionally, and that the whole family had turned on him and on his sister.

This is the devil, he'd thought.

It was something he'd learned about from the boys around the farm. They hadn't learned it in their own church, no. But there were neighbors, non-Amish Christians who had talked about the devil. And the Amish boys were whispering about it, speculating wildly when nobody else was around, especially at night, when they went on secret adventures into the woods together. Yes, there was this thing called the devil, or Satan. It was a man, a force that could take any shape, and which was pure evil. It could appear anywhere and do its work in unimaginable ways. One of the boys would say, "*It could be Teacher Ruthie. It could be your daed or your mamm. It could be one of us right here. It could be* you."

"How do we *know* who the devil is, then?" some boy would eventually ask.

And one of the other boys, the kind who always seems to have the answers, and always seems to have them immediately, would reply, *You know. When the devil shows you his face, you know it.*

Well, Whitey had looked at his father's face, which had been scowling down over him—even as his sister lay dead, even as she was being prepared for burial. He'd looked closely at his father's face as he'd said *Enough foolishness,* and what he saw there wasn't his father's face at all. It was a vacant look. It was the devil. *When the devil shows you his face, you know it.*

Whitey had been sure of it. And his voice, too; it didn't quite sound like his father's voice, especially his tone. This was the devil showing himself. That was the moment Whitey came to believe, with total certainty, that his sister wasn't really dead. That they were burying her alive. As it turned out, he was right about that part. And, to Whitey, being right about that also proved that he was right about his father—that the devil had taken him. Whitey believed that as a boy. And, now, as a grown adult, he still believed it.

Of course, as a child no one believed him about anything. And there was no reason to believe him. The girl was quite clearly dead. Anyone who put their head on her chest could confirm it: there was no heartbeat. Had they kept their ear on her longer, they would have heard it, would have heard the impossibly slow beat, with long pauses between, the sign of her rare condition—but nobody did, and so they drew the natural conclusion. Her heart had stopped.

They ignored Whitey's growing fury. They forgave it and explained it as the pain of a sensitive young boy, unable to reconcile himself with the painful truth. But as he grew more upset, more defiant, more accusatory, and ultimately violent, they began to fear him. Fear what had come over him.

And now that boy, Whitey, fully grown, was taking Rose—whom he had truly come to believe was his sister Hefsibah—down to the creek, to be baptized, and then buried alive. Or, as Whitey referred to it, "to be given over whole," and thus to redeem her forever.

After drying Rose off with a towel, after baptizing her in the creek, after tying up her hair in braids and putting her in a Sunday dress, then gently placing her into an unadorned pine coffin, he could feel the taste of rage rising in him once more.

"How can they *do* this to you?" he roared. "They will *pay*."

That was when he knew he had to contact Ricky and tell his nephew Joseph Young, son of Hezekiah Jonathan Young, about his plan. Let them come here, he thought. Let them suffer, the way that he had suffered. Maybe it would be good for them. Maybe, in this way, they too would be redeemed. He immediately dispatched one of his men to find Ricky and tell him.

And, just like that, in the next moment, his rage completely disappeared, replaced by a painful tenderness toward the girl, and a reverent love. She was a true saint. Look at her! She was meeting her ending without a peep, lying still, waiting, with a serene look on her face. Whitey sobbed heavily, from deep inside himself.

"Don't forget me, Hefsibah. Please remember me," he said between sobs as he closed the top of the coffin.

And after he'd shoveled all the dirt back over the coffin, he'd felt empty. But serene. And then he left.

When Ricky had first arrived at the scene, Whitey's footprints were still crisply impressed into the dirt. It was clear that he'd been there a very short time ago. Maybe just minutes earlier. This was a good sign. It was the closest thing they had to hope.

Not in his wildest dreams could Joseph have envisioned, when he'd told April that "ghost story" about his Amish family, about the girl who was buried alive, that it would end this way, that they would be pulled into this nightmare themselves.

But it was undeniable. None of this would've happened if it wasn't for him. If he hadn't started up with April, Whitey—his estranged uncle—wouldn't have taken this horrible vengeance upon poor Rose. He would have returned her as soon as Ricky had paid up.

The whole ugly reality of the situation hit Joseph,

and it hit him hard. But he also knew that he had to be strong, for April. Now was not a moment for reflection. He threw his full energy into the task of digging, and digging, and digging. If there was one thing he knew how to do, it was that.

April, despite her complete focus on the work that needed to be done, and on her own anxiety and anger and pain and utter horror, still felt a powerful bond with Joseph. There was a signal, some secret invisible channel of communication that existed between them—especially when they were close together—and April could sense that Joseph was suffering.

And not only that. She knew why. She could tell that he blamed himself, and his family, and that he was horrified. Without even looking at him, April could sense what Joseph was thinking. And when she did look at him and read his face, she was certain of it.

For one moment, even as they furiously dug into the ground, April paused and squeezed Joseph's arm, and looked him in the eye. She didn't say a word, and neither did he. It wasn't necessary. Everything was communicated in just that little gesture: Joseph's guilt, April's forgiveness. And the bigger message, too, that each completely understood the other and supported the other completely. It was no more than two seconds between frantic digging—but it was undeniable.

* * *

The ambulance arrived. But when the medics jumped out, ready to go to work, Joseph informed them that they were still digging. The medics stood by, watching in utter disbelief. Next, another van of Ricky's men screeched to a halt beside the shed, almost ramming right into it. The doors flew open and two men jumped out with power shovels.

When April saw the men running toward them, she finally believed that Ricky was, really and truly, on her side. She hadn't quite trusted him at any point, but now she was convinced that he was almost as eager as she was to free Rose from this nightmare. Or at least, to try.

The men dug quickly and efficiently. They didn't exchange a word. There was no need. Everybody knew what needed to be done. And there was also a sense of awe, a kind of hushed understanding that what was happening here, the monstrous burial of a living person and the unburying of wet earth, primal mud, and retrieval into the world of the living, was a kind of sacred, almost mystical act. When people spoke, they whispered. Despite the intense emotions and the heightened adrenaline rush, nobody shouted. For a few minutes the only sound heard was the rhythmic crack and swish of five shovels digging in tandem.

And then, a hollow thud. And then another. This was it. The men picked up their pace, quickly and fervently shoveling out the last layer over the pine coffin, cleaning away the soil from around the edges. Without a second's hesitation, the men threw aside their shovels, and dove into the pit, grabbing the coffin by its sides and hoisting it up and out of the grave, laying it on the ground. That weight, thought April, was the weight of her sister's *body*.

Rose was there. No, Rose was *here*. Right here, right now, just a foot away. April was almost too stunned to breathe, much less move. But she didn't need to: Joseph grabbed her and held her tight, as one of the men fell onto the coffin and quickly jimmied it open.

When they were kids, April and Rose had made a pact. As the elder sister, April had come up with the idea. In order to make absolutely certain that her sister understood what was at stake, she made it as dramatic as possible. They lived in South Philly, near the bridge that crossed the Delaware into New Jersey. There was a park near the bridge and often they went there. One time they'd stood on the bridge together, leaning into the railing. It was a low railing that seemed like something they could easily just hop over, even at ages twelve and ten.

"Would you jump off the bridge for me?" April had asked.

Rose thought about it for a moment, in that serious way of hers. "Yes," she said finally, though with some hesitation. "But it depends."

April had grabbed her sister's jacket and pushed her against the railing, sending her into a panic.

"Depends on *what?*" April had demanded to know.

"On, on—" Rose had struggled. "Like if I jump over . . . does that mean you get saved?"

"Yes," April had said. "That's what I mean."

"Then I would."

"Okay, good," said April, letting go of Rose. And she added, "And I would do the same for you."

But April had never imagined anything like that would ever actually happen. And she had always believed that if someone was going to jump off that bridge, it was going to be April herself. She had never really considered the possibility of losing her sister. Even in these months, when she was certain her sister was gone . . . even then she never really believed that she was *dead*. And now she would do anything—she would, without any hesitation, jump off that bridge to bring Rose back to life.

Unable to move, or breathe, April just stared at the coffin. There was no movement inside and April couldn't bear what her brain was telling her. She couldn't bear to look any longer. Instead she looked at Joseph, trying to read his face as he looked toward the coffin. Based on his reactions, she would try to gauge what was happening inside that coffin.

At first he looked worried, then slightly panicked. It was clear from his face that whatever he was seeing in that coffin was not encouraging. Joseph went over and quickly motioned to Ricky to join him. April desperately wanted to join Joseph too, but she felt literally paralyzed. At just that moment, she felt Carmen's arm wrap around her shoulders.

"I got you, hon," Carmen whispered in April's ear. "I'm right here."

Joseph and Ricky quickly conferred and, without wasting another moment, they reached into the coffin and pulled Rose out, Ricky holding her legs and Joseph hoisting her under her arms. They laid her gently on the ground. She wasn't moving. The medics ran in and immediately got to work.

April felt her own body lose its grip, felt her knees weaken. Carmen tightened her hold on April, keeping her up.

Joseph was on his knees, behind the medics, watching Rose, as they listened for any breath, watching her chest to see if it was moving.

"We gotta do CPR," one of Ricky's men shouted.

"No," one of the medics shouted, "she's breathing."

"You sure?" Joseph said.

The medic hooked Rose onto a monitor, and oxygen. He then turned to Joseph and nodded. Joseph watched a bit more. And then smiled and gave a thumbs-up. And then, in a voice so weary it was almost a whisper, he said, "*She's alive.* Her eyes are open."

Chapter Thirteen

April was starting to grow almost accustomed to the long, bumpy rides in the horse and buggy. It gave her time to think—and it was itself a way of thinking. The journeys were calmingly long and unrushed. But the unpredictable jolts also kept her alert and focused. Even though the buggy was becoming her primary mode of transport, she still couldn't quite believe that this was her life now.

She also couldn't believe—literally could not convince herself that it was real—that, sitting across from her in the buggy, was her sister, Rose. In the past weeks, she'd found herself barely able to feel anything—neither happiness, nor joy, nor even relief. Instead, she found herself simply mesmerized by the physical presence of her sister. She would touch Rose, just take her by the hand, or even lean on her, just to confirm that she was real and alive. Or she would stare at Rose for oddly long periods of time, as though, if she took her eyes off her, Rose would disappear. Wasn't that what had happened before? April would stare like this until Rose gave her a look in return, or said, "Um, can I *help* you?" Sometimes they'd laugh about it. Sometimes it seemed to bother Rose, and she'd just turn away. Rose's moods were hard to predict these days.

Now, in the buggy, April was doing it again. She was staring at Rose. Gazing at her face, almost without blinking. It helped that Rose was asleep, curled up on the corner of the bench, her head resting on her arms.

Seeing Rose asleep unnerved April. It brought her back to that horrible moment when she'd seen the muddy casket. Would she ever unsee that?

She was trying. And succeeding, by degrees. And there were new things to see. Their new home, for instance. Provided for them by Joseph's family. When April had last seen the house, back on that winter night, she'd thought she'd seen the most magical place in her life. And now that she was about to see this same house, months later, in a completely different season, she was certain of it. This place would save her. It would save Rose. It would save her relationship with Joseph. It was amazing grace, was it not? And with the sweet sound of softly swaying willows around it, too.

When talking to Rose, April had been trying not to overpraise the house where they were headed. For one thing, this wasn't a vacation. Rose was going there to heal. She wasn't in any mood to get excited about . . . well, anything. At least not yet. Rose had a long road ahead of her, and April, more than anyone else, knew that. Still, as the buggy made its big turn off the small country highway, onto an unmarked, unpaved road—nothing more than a path through the woods—April suddenly grew excited and could no longer contain it.

"Oh, Rosie," she said, taking her sister's hand in hers, amazed, once again, that she *existed,* and that her hand was so warm. "You're gonna love this place. It's the cutest house ever. It's like *Little House on the Prairie.*"

Rose smiled, quietly. But April couldn't tell exactly what the smile meant, or the quietness, and so she just smiled, too. She didn't say anything more for the moment. It was so odd to be uncertain about her sister's thoughts—the sister whom she knew as well as she knew herself. Usually she could read her mind, finish her thoughts. But things had changed. Rose had been in another world for months. The burial had been an unspeakable experience. A trauma. She was a different person. Quieter, harder to read. April wasn't used to being mystified by Rose, and she had to accustom herself to it, to seeing her sister as a bit of a stranger, to having to get to know her again.

Still, April really did believe that Rose would love this house. If not at first, then definitely with time. And, the good, and great, and completely lucky news was that they actually had time. A lot of it. The house, almost new, was unoccupied. Joseph and his brothers had recently built it for their sister and her new husband, Eli, as a kind of wedding gift for the young couple. But then, just a couple of weeks before they were to move in, the plan had changed. One of Eli's own brothers, back in Wisconsin, suddenly needed help on his dairy—and moving to Wisconsin was something that the couple very much wanted to do. Here was their chance. And their moving out to the Midwest also solved a problem for Joseph's family: Joseph, as the youngest, had had no land, and no home, waiting for him. Now he did, a brand-new one.

But, in the meantime, Joseph gave the home to April and Rose—to give Rose a chance to heal and the sisters time to bond once again. Of course, it also gave Joseph and April a chance to bond again, too. And though Joseph stayed at his cousins' place down the road—*down the road* in Amish terms was quite a bit of distance—he visited the house daily, to help maintain the place, to get some crops going, to help with the chickens, and the other animals they'd brought in. And to check in on Rose. But especially to see his beloved April.

A month passed. Then two. In watching Joseph tend to everything and everyone in the house, every person, goat, horse, and plant, April was reminded of everything she had loved about Joseph. April and Rose, city girls through and through, were learning the ways of country life. They'd wake up very early, almost at dawn. By the time April was making breakfast, the roosters would be crowing. Their morning scrambled eggs came from their own hens; the apple jam for their toast came from a nearby orchard.

Rose, in particular, had taken to preserving and canning fruit. Joseph's sisters taught her how to do it. The repetitive nature of the work comforted her. Filling jar after jar with sweet stuff made her happy. She felt a sense of accomplishment in watching the pantry fill up with glowing jars of pink and green and dark rose-red. It made her feel safe to see a full pantry, especially with winter coming. All of those pretty jars hinted at a future. Each jar represented a week in the future that belonged to her, and sharing meals with the people she loved. Each jar took her further away from the pain of the past. Rose never said that. But April knew her sister. And when she watched her at work, canning the jam and placing a new jar in the pantry, she could see it all plainly.

The remainder of the day would be dedicated to tending the farm. Inspecting the crops. Watering and pruning. Securing fences and digging ditches. Tending to the animals. Feeding and grooming them, clearing their enclosures, harvesting eggs from the coops. And when all of the chores were done for the day, the sisters would help Joseph, who was building a granary and storage silo. Occasionally they'd make a trip to the store. And then it was time to make a fire and cook dinner. By the end of the day, April and Rose would be sitting around the fire, mending clothes, cleaning up, and entertaining each other. The cat would be dozing nearby.

"Look at us," Rose said one evening as they sat there.

"What do you mean?" asked April.

"Look around here," Rose said, sweeping her hand around the cabin. "How did we become *Amish?* Like, *what?*"

April giggled, and Rose continued.

"Like, how are you *sewing?* You don't know how to sew!"

"Actually," April replied, "you're right. I really don't."

She held up the shirt she'd been sewing, one of Joseph's, and displayed a ridiculously crooked and messy seamline. They burst out laughing.

"We suck at being Amish," Rose said, with tears streaming down her face. It was the first time April had seen her sister laugh like that, or cry. Since she'd returned, she had shown very little open emotion. But now that corner had been turned. And, for a moment, a small tear came to April's eyes, too.

April was particularly taken by the care that Joseph was showing to her sister. He always asked April about her progress and listened very carefully to her answers. He spent a lot of time teaching Rose, gently and patiently, how to tend the farm. And even better than teaching, he listened attentively to her. He watched her, with his special intuitive glances, to see what things she seemed excited to do, and he focused on those things. When he saw that she was interested in preserving and canning fruit, he came back the next day with extra bushels of apples, grapes, and berries, and jars. An entire buggy-ful of supplies.

"Do we really need *that* much?" April had whispered to Joseph when Rose had gone out to begin unloading everything from the buggy.

"No," Joseph had replied. "We don't. But Rose does."

And later, when the jars were starting to pile up, Joseph suggested that his cousin would be happy to sell the surplus jam at the market. Rose immediately brightened up, excited that her labor would bring in some money. When Rose seemed to want a new task, Joseph would make suggestions. And when Rose seemed to want solitude, he'd let her be. April watched all of this, constantly impressed, constantly moved.

Once, sitting around the fire at night, after a long busy day during the last corn harvest in late fall, Rose had mentioned that she'd always wanted a big brown dog. She knew that she'd call this big brown dog Darlene. The next day, Joseph showed up with a small picnic basket.

"Look who I found," he'd said, as he walked in

and placed the basket down on the table, where April had been setting up breakfast.

Joseph took full advantage of his understated manner to set up the surprise. So much so that Rose, still half-asleep, hardly noticed that the basket was lined with roses, whose de-thorned stems were braided together into a little nest that held a tiny, tiny puppy whose eyes were so big they seemed to be half her size. A little handmade sign that read DARLENE dangled from her neck.

"Darlene!" Rose said, with a big sleepy smile.

And the moment she said it, Darlene's tiny tail began wagging. All that day, Darlene didn't leave Rose's side, or maybe Rose didn't leave Darlene's side. But they were inseparable from then on. When Joseph said that he'd got the puppy from a "farm right down the road," he neglected to mention, until April pulled it out of him privately later, that he'd actually traveled three hours each way, to a farm in the next county, to pick Darlene up. And this was after spending almost the entire day inquiring after puppies. April watched all of this, watched how Joseph gently helped heal her sister, and with each passing day, her love for Joseph deepened.

April and Joseph were spending more time together. More than ever before. No matter how early April woke up, Joseph was always already in the house, waiting patiently for her. Around the farm,

Joseph was an endless flurry of activity. Lying in bed in the morning, before dawn, April could hear Joseph downstairs, puttering around in his stocking feet on the hardwood floor, trying hard not to make too much noise.

She found his sounds comforting. Often, she spent a few extra minutes in bed, just listening to him organizing and dusting and fixing things. Each little act of domestic upkeep was, to her, a kind of small kiss or a love letter. He never made a big deal of it. And only shrugged when she thanked him. But he was constant in his efforts to help her and Rose, to make their lives easier and safer and more comfortable.

How was it possible that just a few months ago she didn't trust him? All of that distrust and misunderstanding now seemed so far in the past. It wasn't even the past. It was another life. And now, in retrospect, it all seemed so clear. Yes, she'd been under a lot of stress, and confused, because of Rose's disappearance. She was right to question, to suspect Joseph and pretty much everything else in her life at that point. And yet, the deeper reason she hadn't trusted him was simpler than that. It had more to do with April herself, her past: she had never been with a man like Joseph.

She'd never had a man in her life whom she could trust completely and who went out of his way to be there for her. She hadn't believed it was possible. Why would she? There had to be another explanation for all of Joseph's compassionate labors. It couldn't be what it looked like. But now, it was clear: it was what it looked like. April knew that. In growing to trust Joseph, she was really growing to trust herself, her own judgments, her own perceptions.

On the farm, day in and day out, April was feeling something in her change. She was noticing things about herself. Some hardened exterior was falling away from her. She hadn't ever recognized it as a hardened exterior. She'd always just thought of it as a part of herself. Part of everyone. But it turned out it wasn't. And when it fell away, leaving her exposed, soft and vulnerable, she somehow didn't feel any less safe. On the contrary, it was an unprecedented feeling of safety that allowed her to drop the shield away. This was her truer self, and it feared nothing.

She felt a literal weight had been lifted from her. She felt lighter and freer than she'd ever felt before. She would occasionally just jump up on her toes because she felt so light. *This was what joy must feel like,* she thought to herself. Joy wasn't just some idea. It was a very real physical state: it felt like gravity somehow didn't totally apply to her. It made everything in the world feel warmer, gentler. It made her notice things more. Notice people. And be kinder. It let her sleep better, eat better. Not until she'd dropped the shield—the shield that she'd been holding her entire life—did she realize how much it hurt her body to hold it up all the time, causing tension in her arms and back and neck. But now the shield had been set aside and, with it, the pain of holding it.

But with all the small joys, of new love, and of growing family, nobody dared say the name of the man who had kidnapped and almost killed Rose. It was critical to Rose's recovery that she not hear the name Whitey, that she not dwell on the experience she'd just endured. Not until she recovered from the ordeal, not until years of peace had passed. Maybe never.

And yet, thoughts about Whitey were not far from anyone's minds. How could they not be? He was still out there. April thought about that. And so did Carmen. Joseph definitely thought about him. Occasionally, when Rose was elsewhere, April would whisper to Joseph about Whitey, about the fact that he was still at large. With the passing weeks and months, it seemed less and less likely that the police would bring him to justice.

And, they all knew, too, the dark reason why he was still free. He was an FBI asset, valuable as an informant to the feds. And so Whitey remained a free man, on the loose, somewhere out there, maybe not too far away.

There wasn't much anyone could do but worry about it. And equal to this fear was their concern about shielding Rose from their fears. Though they never brought it up with her, occasionally she herself would say something. Once, in a panic, in the middle of the night, Rose had jolted from sleep and shocked

April awake. "We need to *do* something. We need to leave!" Rose had said urgently.

She had been inconsolable that night. Even when April managed to calm Rose, to soothe her, and convince her that she was safe, Rose kept saying, "People don't know. They don't *know*. They don't realize how dangerous he is." April didn't disagree. And yet, it was important that Rose herself let go of this knowledge, and work to build a new life apart from these dark, late-night fears.

Fortunately, that new life was taking form, every day, slowly. One day, Joseph announced that they would host a barn raising on their new farm. The entire community would come over and build them a barn in the span of a couple days.

This made April nervous. As Joseph had explained it to her, the raising of a barn wasn't just about the barn, or about helping out a particular family farm, it was about coming together as a community. It was about seeing each other, gossiping, sharing food, and having fun. He called it "a frolic"—which April had thought was a joke, until Joseph explained that this was actually the word the Amish used for it. As Joseph said, "It's about getting in a good visit, y'know?"

Barn raisings, or frolics, happened less frequently these days than in the past. Joseph couldn't even remember the last time he'd seen one.

"It's high time," Joseph had said. "Folks want it for the community more than for us," he explained. "We owe it to them."

Which was exactly why April was nervous about it. She wasn't exactly a normal member of this community yet, and the idea of the frolic stressed her out. Though people had been enormously kind to her, she couldn't help but feel that these acts of kindness always highlighted the basic fact that she was an outsider in a vulnerable position. Wouldn't this event put the spotlight on April even more? It was one thing to manage the stares when she showed up at the Amish general store, or when she and Joseph rode by folks in their horse and buggy. But to have the entire community *all together* staring at her? It was just too daunting for April to consider. And she was also worried about Rose, who was still in a delicate stage of her recovery. Rose didn't need the stress.

"A frolic?" Rose said, when April told her about it. "That sounds so *fun!*"

And, just like that, April no longer had Rose's reaction as an excuse. Quite the opposite. Rose had clearly brightened up at the idea. The barn raising would be good for her, and so now April had no choice but to agree to it.

The day of the barn raising was even more stressful than April had imagined. She had woken up early to bake all the bread, and to prepare massive pots of stew to feed the hungry workers. April was so harried, running around checking on boiling pots and hot ovens, that she barely noticed when Rose emerged from the staircase in Amish "Plain" dress, complete with bonnet.

"What do you think?" Rose said, finally.

"I didn't even see it was you," April said.

"Figured I'd give it a whirl," Rose said. "See how it feels. I kind of like the bonnet thing . . . it makes it easier to hide if you wanna roll your eyes at someone."

"I'm not sure you're really catching on to this Amish thing," April said.

"But seriously," Rose said, "what do you think?"

"Seriously?" April said. "You really shouldn't, Rosie. Not now. It's a big deal to wear that. We're still guests here."

"Ugh, fine," Rose said, as she retreated back up the stairs to change.

"Just gimme a day or two with it," Rose replied. "I'll get it."

"Oh, I know you will."

They both laughed, because they both knew it was true. Rose was famous in their family for being a chameleon.

As soon as the frolic began, Rose immediately made friends with some of the Amish girls, who marveled at her tenacity while playing badminton.

"I play to *win!*" Rose exclaimed, raising a fist after scoring a point, and then realized that maybe she should tone it down just a bit. But the girls giggled and loved her enthusiasm.

And not just the girls. Rose was getting all kinds of looks from the gentlemen, all of whom were supposed to be working hard on raising the barn. But between their labors, hauling wood and nailing boards together, they shot her looks and whispered amongst themselves.

A certain young man, Samuel Jenner, seemed particularly attentive, never failing to make a wide looping detour to the picnic tables where Rose sat with April and the other women. By the third time he made one of these near visits, trying hard to look at Rose without being seen to look—and all the while supposedly gathering more nails for the barn—the women were laughing at him.

"How many nails does he need?" someone said, and everyone laughed.

Later, this same Samuel finally approached Rose directly. Boldly he asked her if she wanted to be on his badminton team, and she got a close look at his dimples and his cute little smile and his curls peeking out of his jaunty cap. And, in between points in the badminton game, she and April, who was sitting nearby watching, exchanged meaningful looks.

And even as April gave her sister sly looks, and barely suppressed her giggles, she, in her heart, was giving thanks to God—yes, God, a new interest of hers—that her sister had been saved and that she could still smile at life and be herself. After everything that had happened, Rose could still be playful and hopeful about the future. How could April not give thanks for that? And as Rose laughed at Samuel's bad jokes and blushed at his long glances, there was ample reason, too, to be hopeful about Rose's future.

As Rose healed and grew stronger, April could turn more of her attention to Joseph. He was very happy to have it. They would go on long walks. At the end of each morning, after the chores were done, April would roll up her apron and go outside, where she'd find Joseph leaning his strong body against the stone well, drying his hands on his pants, smiling at her. Darlene, whose small puppy body hadn't quite caught up with her long legs and paws, would immediately run out with her tail wagging madly, knowing what was about to happen. And April knew she'd never been happier in her life.

They'd walk through the fields while Joseph listened carefully to everything April said—and looked at her even more carefully, to read those things she wasn't saying. He'd also keep one eye on the crops as they passed by. Often, they would stop while Joseph made an adjustment to some of the wiring on the tomato plants, or to give April a quick agricultural tutorial on something that was happening with a plant. On the farm, the work never ended. But it didn't feel endless; the work was folded into life, folded into their day-to-day, minute-to-minute existence without much thought, like breathing. Once they reached the end of the field, they would continue on into the woods, onto the little path that Joseph had blazed just for April.

These little walks brought Joseph and April back to their earliest days together, even before they were together. Like those walks a year earlier, they spoke openly with each other, in a spirit of trust and curiosity. The more they got reacquainted and the more they got to know each other, the more they realized that there was so much more to learn and know.

But unlike those early walks around Philly, back when April was working at the Metropolitan Bakery and Joseph at the Amish diner, they weren't being watched or rushed. Out here, on the farm, they could do as they pleased, without prying eyes, and they needn't rush back to their jobs—though, of course, the needs of farmwork were never too far from their minds.

In Philly, their time together was always cursed by the awareness that what they were doing was a bit wrong, impossible. That there was no future for them. All of that had changed. Now, on the farm, they spoke about the future; they dreamed together.

One afternoon, they made their way through the cornfields, shielded by the high stalks of the late harvest. As they walked by the stalks, Joseph was peeling off top layers of the corn husks, and braiding them together into a kind of rope. After a few moments, April posed the obvious question, which neither had yet asked.

"What changed?" April said.

"What do you mean?" asked Joseph, peeling off more husks, and expertly tying them together. "'*Changed*'—with what?"

He knows exactly what I mean, April thought.

"With us," she said.

"Everything," Joseph said. "Everything changed. But I always wanted to be together."

"But why do you think things will work out for us now, when before you didn't?"

Joseph thought about it for a moment.

"Is it because I'm getting into the Amish thing?" April said.

"That helps," Joseph replied. "But it's more than that. . . . We've been through so much together now."

They walked for a bit, without a word.

"You know this isn't going to be easy," Joseph said. "I've been speaking to my family, and we've come to some understandings. But some of my family may never accept you, no matter what you do. My community has been welcoming so far because our situation now is so unusual. And because we know, better than anyone, what it means to be a victim of Whitey. But, in the long run, they might not accept us. We might have to move out of Pennsylvania, to a community that will be more open to us. This could be a long road. And it won't be easy."

April nodded.

"Nothing I've ever done has been easy," April

said. "But I want to try it. And you know . . . if your community doesn't accept me, well, mine will accept you. How would you feel about that?"

Joseph didn't reply right away.

"If it comes to that . . . I want to be with you," he said, finally. "You are my community."

They walked together silently for a moment. All the while, Joseph peeled more husks, and expertly braided them into his little sculpture.

"Joseph?"

"Yes?"

"Are you asking me—"

But before she could finish the thought, Joseph had stopped and gotten down on both knees. He took her hand and tugged her down, too, so that she also was on both knees. He now presented his corn husk creation, which turned out to be an intricately braided little crown. He placed it on her head.

"It fits *perfectly*," she said. "How did you do that? That's just creepy. . . ."

"*Shhhh*," he said. "April, will you marry me?"

The moment she said yes, his lips were already on hers, warm and strong. After a long, head-swimming kiss he leaned in and whispered something in her ear, something that was only for her to hear, and which she would never, as long as she lived, forget.

The next week, on a Friday, April could tell that something was up. Joseph had said that he needed some extra help damming part of a creek and enlisted

April's help. After a few hours of work, chopping wood, and rearranging stones, it started to get dark and Joseph announced that it was time to return home. April was exhausted from the work, and from waking up that morning before dawn. Sitting on Joseph's horse, clutching on to Joseph as the horse walked carefully along the forest path, April fell asleep and stayed that way despite the bumps and lurches.

When they arrived back at the house, April, slightly refreshed from her nap, walked toward the house first, eager for dinner. Especially when the aromas of what smelled like a feast reached her on the steps up to the porch. The moment the door opened, everything became clear at once.

Surprrrrrise!

She saw Carmen first, and their eyes met. Then she saw Joseph's family, his brothers and sister, *daed* and *mamm,* uncles and aunts. Then she saw her own sister, Rose, beaming, and looking healthy and very much like her old self. And then April turned and saw Joseph.

"So that's why you dragged me out to 'build a dam'!" she said.

"We needed you out of the house," Rose said, "while we prepared everything."

And then Joseph leaned closer to April. "Can I tell them?" he whispered, pointing to his ring finger. April smiled and nodded. Joseph took April's hand in his, and said, "Hey, everyone! Can I get your attention please? We have some news to share. It's good news! I promise. . . ."

Please read on for a preview
of the sequel to

SEARCHING FOR ROSE,

coming soon!

Rose lay in bed, perfectly still, eyes wide open. Sometimes, at night, at the end of a long, exhausting day on the farm, her body would sink into a grateful sleep, but her eyes remained wide open. At least, that was how it felt to her. There would be images and voices so vivid, they could only be real. Images whose undeniable realness, however, evaporated the moment she found herself waking up in the morning, and realized it was all a dream.

But this time, it wasn't. She lay in bed, truly awake, her eyes wide open. These sounds were real. They had to be. They were coming from outside her window. The dog was barking. This wasn't a dream.

She rolled out of bed, crouched by the window, and peered out the bottom corner of it, careful to keep her head outside the frame. Across the way, she saw the two small windows of the barn squinting back at her like dark, empty eyes. The buggy stood next to the barn door in its usual spot. The barn door was half-open, which was not usual. In front of the barn, the lawn was empty. But it was a shimmering, charged emptiness, a vibrating darkness.

Something ran by. Rose heard the rapid footsteps. She saw a blur. Now the dog was barking even louder. She raised her head a bit. She needed both eyes. She was barely breathing or blinking. She didn't want to miss it, whatever it was. Something was out there. Someone. There were nights, and even sometimes during the day, when she was certain he was near. Sometimes, in the fields, she was certain that she was being watched. She could feel it in her body. In her joints. In the little hairs on the back of her neck.

She'd moved out to this farm, with her sister and her soon-to-be brother-in-law, in the middle of the country, to heal. And, slowly, it was working. But there were moments of backsliding, of relapse. Of utter fear. The healing was slow, but the backsliding . . . that would happen rapidly, and without warning, like an ambush. One moment the slow comforts of health buoyed her, and the next, she was suddenly thrown into the middle of a foaming, frigid sea, thrashing about, choking on saltwater, drowning.

At other times, the experience was something else altogether, something beyond even fear.

She saw the boot first. For one brief second, it flashed next to the barn door, and was gone. But she'd seen it. Her heart raced. Someone was in there.

The feelings suddenly took over. The feelings she never told anyone about. The feelings she barely admitted to herself.

It's him, she thought. *Who else?*

And the feeling that came with that thought wasn't fear or dread or horror. Rather, it was the feeling that lurked on the other side of fear; it was where fear leaves you when it is done with you. It was agitation and excitement. It was the painful pleasure of anticipation. And with it, a spiral of irrational thoughts. *He's come for me. He promised he would, and now he's making good on it. They say he's evil. But I know the truth. He's special. He sees me for who I am. He'll bring me back to the Compound. Back to the Community. Back* home.

For a moment Rose savored these secret thoughts, savored this moment, allowed her heart to clench with anticipation at the thought that she would be restored to the good graces of Whitey. She stood up and set herself squarely in the middle of the window, to see better. Who cared if he saw her? Rose *wanted* to be seen. She stared out the window. She bored her eyes into that barn door, trying to will it open, to reveal him, to reveal herself to him.

I'm here, she whispered in the dark, to him.

She considered turning around, running downstairs, and flying out the door. Running to him and taking nothing with her. Begging for his forgiveness, begging to be brought back home.

"*Rose.*"

She jumped, and bumped her head against the window frame.

"Didn't mean to startle you," April said, standing behind her, leaning against the doorpost.

"It's okay," Rose said over her shoulder, but still looking outside.

Outside, the fullness of the dark had drained away. It no longer shimmered. Now it just seemed empty and quiet on the lawn. And Rose's secret thoughts evaporated, too. For a brief, lucid second, she felt guilty about her excitement to see Whitey again. But just as quickly the guilt was also gone—forgotten, as though it, and the thoughts that caused it, had never existed to begin with. It was as if she had just woken up and immediately forgotten the dream she was having.

Seeing her sister's tired, worried face brought her back to the moment. She smiled.

"Don't worry, Ri," Rose said. "Just having some trouble sleeping."

And when she saw the skeptical, sad look on her sister's face, she added, "I'm *fine*. Really. I'm okay. I'll be asleep in a minute. You don't need to tuck me in."

"Joseph said he saw you looking out the window," April said.

"Oh, that was him out there. Well, I'm allowed to look out the window, right?"

"He said you looked . . ." April didn't finish the sentence, and seemed to regret bringing it up.

"Tired?" said Rose. "Well, yeah, I am. And, anyway, maybe I was looking out the window because your dude was creeping around in the middle of the night."

April sighed.

"You're right. He shouldn't do that."

"What was he doing out there?"

"We—or, I . . . tonight was my night—I forgot to

secure the coop. Joe saw a coyote out there, and ran over to get things right before there was trouble. Got there just in time."

After they said their good-nights, Rose climbed back into bed. And just as she drifted off to sleep, she heard voices. It was April again, and Joseph. She could hear their voices coming through the grate in the floor. They must have been in the kitchen, right below her room. Her body was heavy, and already succumbing to sleep. But her head guided itself to the edge of the bed. She flopped over, facedown, so that her ear was poised right at the edge.

"So," she heard April say, "what was it?"

And then Joseph's lower voice, muffled, said something.

"Are you sure?" April said. "It was *him?*"

Joseph coughed. He either didn't answer, or he was pausing, or Rose simply couldn't hear him. Rose could feel herself drifting headlong into sleep.

"I don't know," Joseph said. She was struggling to stay awake. And, as sleep finally carried her away, she thought she heard him add, "But it was someone."

Connect with Us

Visit us online at
KensingtonBooks.com
to read more from your favorite authors, see books
by series, view reading group guides, and more.

Join us on social media

for sneak peeks, chances to win books and prize packs,
and to share your thoughts with other readers.

facebook.com/kensingtonpublishing
twitter.com/kensingtonbooks

Tell us what you think!

To share your thoughts, submit a review,
or sign up for our eNewsletters, please visit:
KensingtonBooks.com/TellUs.